THE PHANT

Also by Peter Read

Diamond Mine (The Book Guild)
The Peking Diamonds (Gembooks)

Gemmological Instruments (Butterworths)
Beginner's Guide to Gemmology (Heinemann)
Gems — Questions and Answers (Heinemann)
Dictionary of Gemmology (Butterworths)
Gemmology (Butterworth-Heinemann)

PETER READ

The *PHANTOM DIAMOND*

GEMBOOKS
1996

First published 1996 by
Gembooks
16 Green Park
Manor Road
Bournemouth
Dorset

ISBN 0-9525315-1-8

Cover photograph by courtesy of R V Huddlestone

British Library in Publication Data. A catalogue record of this book is available from the British Library.

Typeset in New Century 10/12pt by Scriptmate Editions
Manufacture coordinated in UK by Book-in-Hand Ltd
20 Shepherds Hill, London N6 5AH

To my wife Joan for her constructive criticisms,
suggestions and corrections,
and to my friend Frank for his expert proof reading
of the manuscript

Author's Foreword

The Phantom Diamond is the third part of my Diamond Trilogy, which includes the two previous novels *Diamond Mine* and *The Peking Diamonds*. All three stories are thrillers set in the mining, marketing and manufacturing world of diamonds. Although the books are self-contained, and can be read in any order, this third novel features characters, and refers to events, from the two previous books. For new readers, the following brief synopses of the two earlier books will set the scene for events which take place in this volume.

Diamond Mine — A massive new diamond discovery in the ageing Pretoria Mine threatens to reduce the production quota of the rival Coastal Diamond Corporation's operation on the windswept beaches at Edeldorp in Namibia. CDC's Security Director, Clive Drake, plans to destroy the new workings at the Pretoria Mine, and employs mercenaries to hijack an explosive device recently developed by South Africa's defence force. Christine Keogh, the mine's PR officer, and Mike Reece, the mine's underground manager, are caught up in a dangerous web of passion, intrigue, treachery and murder as the story races towards an explosive conclusion.

The Peking Diamonds — In one of the world's largest uncut diamond marketing organisations, security cameras record suspicious activities on the sorting benches. Three diamond sorters are dismissed, but all three are then found dead in suspicious circumstances. Paul Remington, head of the Diamond Syndicate's Special Operations section, and his assistant Steven Heming, begin an investigation which uncovers a Russian plot to take over the Syndicate's clients. The plot has been masterminded by the head of the Soviet Foreign Trade Association, and is backed by Colonel Leo Vessovski, head of the KGB. The trail of death leads from the Syndicate's diamond sorting offices in London, to Moscow, Hong Kong, Peking and the waterways and massage parlours of Bangkok. As the investigation draws to a conclusion, Paul Remington and Stephanie Goddard, secretary to Sir James, the Syndicate's Chairman, unwittingly involve their South African friends, Mike and Christine Reece, and their young daughter Melanie, in the dangerous climax. After several clashes with KGB agents, and a kidnapping, the story culminates in a SAS-style rescue.

Contents

PREFACE

In 1898, in the north east corner of South Africa's Cape Province, Thomas Cullinan, a one-time bricklayer, had been working for several years as a builder in and around the diamond town of Kimberley. The growing town was at the height of its diamond fever and his services were in constant demand, enabling him to build up a modest fortune.

Cullinan became familiar with some of the geological aspects of diamond prospecting. He was aware, for example, of the appearance of the small rounded hills called kopjes which sometimes formed the remains of a diamond-bearing volcanic eruption, and while visiting Pretoria in the Transvaal he decided to spend some time prospecting for diamonds. One day, twenty miles north-east of Pretoria, he met a man who showed him a three-carat diamond he had picked up nearby on a farm. When he visited the site of the farm Cullinan noticed a kopje that reminded him of Kimberley's small hills, and he immediately tried to buy the farm. The old Boer farmer had already been driven off two previous farms where first gold and then diamonds had been found. This had made the old man stubbornly resolved not to move again — even when Cullinan offered him a generous price.

Thomas Cullinan was not a man to give up easily. Despite the declaration of war on Britain by the Boer President Paul Kruger in 1899 and the two-year siege of Kimberley that followed, he maintained his interest in the acquisition of the farm. His persistence eventually paid off. The siege of Kimberley was finally broken in 1900, the farmer died, and Cullinan was at last able to buy the farm from the old man's daughter.

As soon as the farm was his, Cullinan lost no time in having the whole area surrounding the kopje prospected, and by 1903 the hill that had attracted his attention five years earlier was identified as the top of the biggest diamond pipe discovered so far. Two years later on the site of the farm there was a giant excavation — the Premier Mine was in production.

Late in the afternoon of January 25 1905, the heat of the high veld summer day was beginning to subside and the golden rays of the setting sun were bathing the eastern perimeter of the great open-cast pit of the Premier Mine. The mine's surface manager, Frederick Wells, a stocky man in his early forties, was completing his routine end-of-the-day inspection of the mine's working level. The shadow cast by the western wall of the pit had already reached halfway to where Frederick was standing. He shielded his eyes from the glare of the orange-red sun and watched a string of trucks loaded with mined rock being hauled by a small locomotive to the treatment plant just beyond the perimeter of the pit.

As he turned to continue his tour of inspection his attention was suddenly caught by a flash of light. Something halfway up the face of the eastern rock wall was reflecting the rays of the dying sun. Picking his way across the rough terrain he moved to a spot which he judged to be just below the reflecting object and peered up at the rock face. A few feet above his head he could see something bright protruding from the surface of the jagged side wall. He caught hold of a projecting ledge and heaved himself up the sloping rock surface. Using his pocket knife he carefully prised out what seemed to be a lump of glass. The semi-transparent object was about the size of his fist and felt surprisingly heavy. He put the find carefully in his pocket and lowered himself to the working surface.

By now the sun had set below the mine's perimeter. Frederick walked back towards the cluster of buildings on the west side of the pit and joined a group of black labourers heading for the security search compound at the end of their working day. He climbed the ramp that led out of the pit and walked swiftly across to the mine's administration building. William McHardy, the tall bearded general manager, was still in his office and together they examined the find under an inspection lamp. The semi-transparent object measured nearly four inches long by two and a half inches thick, and weighed over 600 grams. A careful hardness test proved beyond doubt that the find was diamond and not glass, and Thomas Cullinan (now Sir Thomas Cullinan) who happened to be visiting the mine that day was immediately informed of the startling discovery.

The following day Sir Thomas posed for an historic photograph beside his two managers who jointly held the soon-to-be famous diamond. The largest uncut diamond in the world, verified as weighing 3,024 carats (3,106 carats by the later metric standard), was sent by ox cart with the rest of the previous week's diamond recovery to the local railway station. From here it was dispatched to the Premier Mine's offices in Johannesburg.

The diamond was named the Cullinan. Although the stone became world-famous and was displayed all over Europe, it soon became an embarrassment to the Premier Mining Company. In the depressed state of the diamond market no-one wanted to buy it. However, two years later it was finally purchased by the Transvaal Government for £150,000. On the 9th of November 1907, as a gesture of reconciliation to the British nation after the Boer war, it was presented to King Edward VII on his 66th birthday.

The King decided to have the stone cut and polished, but at that time there were few diamantaires who had ever handled a diamond of more than a few hundred carats. Eventually the King entrusted it to the well-known company of Asscher's in Amsterdam, which had earlier been responsible for cutting the 995.2 carat Excelsior diamond as well as several other important large gems.

In order to produce the best yield of polished diamonds from the large Cullinan stone, it was studied for nearly six months before the final decisions were made and the surface of the gem marked for cleaving. First of all a V-shaped groove was cut along the direction of the diamond's cleavage 'grain'. Then, on February 10 1908, surrounded by members of his staff, Mr Asscher picked up a steel cleaver's blade and placed it carefully in the groove. Using a heavy steel rod he struck the blade a sharp blow. To his dismay, the blade broke in two, but the diamond remained in one piece.

He selected another blade, and at the second attempt the big diamond split in two as planned. A second groove was then cut in the smaller of the two resulting halves, and this was also cleaved in two to produce a total of three separate pieces. Over the next few months, these were cleaved and sawn into nine major diamonds, ninety-six smaller stones, and over nine carats of small unpolished chips.

The largest of the principal stones, the Cullinan I, was a pear-shaped gem weighing 530.2 carats and was later known as the Star of Africa. The next largest, the Cullinan II, weighed 317.4 carats and was cushion-shaped. It was called the Second Star of Africa. Both of these stones were on show in the Jewel House at the Tower of London in 1908. In 1909 the Cullinan II was set in the imperial state crown just below the Black Prince Ruby, and in 1910 the royal sceptre was remade to take the Cullinan I.

Despite the alarming events which occurred towards the end of the twentieth century, some of which are revealed here for the first time, the Cullinan I, which to a select few became known as the 'Phantom Diamond', is now re-mounted in the royal sceptre and is on view to the public among the royal regalia in the Tower of London's new Jewel House.

CHAPTER 1

SYDNEY
Saturday 18 October, 1980

The security guard inside the entrance to Sydney's Lower Town Hall in George Street laid a restraining hand on the arm of a young girl carrying a large dress box.

'I'm sorry, Miss, but you'll have to check that in at reception.'

'But it's my wedding dress,' objected the girl. 'I've just collected it — I'd rather miss the exhibition than let this out of my sight.'

The guard sighed. 'OK, but I'll have to check the contents.'

The girl pulled the lid off the box and lifted up the tissue paper. 'Do you think it'll suit me?'

'No worries there, Miss — it'll go a treat with those lacy gloves you're wearing.' He smiled and waved her in. 'Enjoy the show.'

The jewellery exhibition in the Hall had been well publicised, particular emphasis being placed on the rare chance for the public to see the Golconda d'Or, one of the world's largest golden yellow diamonds. The emerald-cut 95.4 carat diamond, owned by the Sydney jewellery firm of Angus and Coote, and lent by them to the exhibition organisers, was said to be worth more than £250,000. Aside from these statistics, the stone was equally famous for being one of the last of the large diamonds recovered from the legendary Golconda mines in eighteenth-century India, a country which for many years had been the main source of the world's diamonds.

The girl carrying the dress box purchased a catalogue at the reception desk and strolled into the Hall's exhibition room. It was nearly midday and the spring temperature outside the Hall had reached a moderate 20 degrees. Inside the air-conditioned exhibition room weekend shoppers and tourists were enjoying the display of expensive jewellery. At the far end of the room, well separated from the rest of the exhibition pieces, a polished wooden plinth supported a square glass display cabinet. Inside the cabinet the Golconda d'Or diamond was mounted on a stand placed in the middle of a rotating pedestal. Four small spotlights illuminated the gem and generated flashes of rainbow hued light from its facets as the stone slowly rotated.

To stop the viewing public touching the glass cabinet, a rope barrier had been placed around the wooden plinth. Just before twelve o'clock a well-dressed man squeezed through the group of people admiring the Golconda d'Or. As the man leaned forward over the rope to get a closer look, one of the four pillars holding up the rope toppled over.

A security guard moved swiftly forward and righted the pillar. 'Now take it easy, mate,' he warned. 'Just keep behind the barrier, or you'll get me fired!' The guard hovered by the display cabinet for a few minutes until the group viewing the large diamond began to thin out. Then he moved away to circulate among the other displays.

The young girl holding the dress box had been watching the guard. She turned and signalled to someone behind her in the crowd, and then sauntered casually towards the roped-off display cabinet. Two men, followed by a middle-aged woman, joined her in front of the Golconda diamond. The shorter of the two men slipped on a pair of flesh-coloured linen gloves. 'Cover me,' he whispered to his companion, and strolled around to the far side of the cabinet.

The middle-aged woman turned round and engaged the girl in conversation while the second man kept a sharp lookout for the security guard and was ready to create a diversion if needed. Meanwhile, the man wearing the gloves stepped quickly over the rope barrier and knelt down behind the cabinet. He unscrewed the rear panel of the wooden plinth and squeezed inside the plinth. Using a skeleton key he reached up and picked the lock at the base of the display case door. Seconds later he emerged from the plinth and replaced the rear panel. He stood up cautiously and glanced at the young girl on the far side of the display unit. She nodded to him, opened her dress box and held it up in front of the glass case as if showing its contents to her companion. At that precise moment, the man wearing the gloves opened the cabinet's glass door, took the Golconda d'Or from its stand on the rotating pedestal and put it in his pocket. Then he pulled an amber coloured glass replica from another pocket and quickly placed it on the empty stand.

'What are you doing?'

The man looked up in surprise at the elderly grey-haired woman who had suddenly appeared at the side of the display cabinet. 'I was fixing the rotating pedestal,' he replied, closing the cabinet's glass door. 'It kept sticking.'

Her curiosity satisfied, the elderly woman moved away. The lookout man breathed a sigh of relief. He turned and walked slowly towards the exit door followed by the young girl and the middle-aged woman. The remaining member of the gang took off his linen gloves, stuffed them in his pocket and climbed back over the rope barrier. He glanced at his watch and smiled to himself. The whole operation had taken just three minutes.

A short while later, someone noticed that the 'gem' in the display case had fallen off its stand. One of the security guards was called over, and he immediately contacted the organisers. It took several more precious seconds to open up the glass cabinet and for a diamond expert to confirm their worst suspicions — the Golconda d'Or had been stolen. The exit doors were immediately locked and the police alerted.

Within minutes a team from the Sydney crime squad arrived. Everyone in the room was searched and interviewed, and the room was combed for clues. No fingerprints were found on either the display unit or the glass replica. The police did however find a cardboard box containing the wedding dress and a pair of lace gloves under a car in a nearby side street. Although they managed to trace the bridal shop that had sold the dress, they found it had been purchased by a man who paid in cash. The description of the man tallied with that of the lookout, but there the trail ended.

Among the witnesses interviewed, the security guard at the entrance thought that the girl carrying the dress box had a South African accent. The elderly woman who talked to the man behind the glass display case, thought he had a Polish accent.

The police later issued a statement in which they pointed out that the thieves would have difficulty in selling the diamond as it was so well known. It was in fact rated No.51 in order of size in the list of the world's polished diamonds.

From descriptions provided by one of the security guards and two members of the public, photofit pictures and other details of the gang of four were later circulated around Australia and sent overseas through Interpol. The Golconda d'Or was never seen again, and it was assumed it had either been recut into several smaller stones and disposed of without arousing suspicion, or was still intact but lay in some wealthy collector's private vault.

CHAPTER 2

LONDON
Thirteen years later — Tuesday 14 September, 1993

Steven walked down Victoria Embankment towards Westminster Bridge. The afternoon was fine and sunny, and he paused for a moment to view the broad expanse of the Thames as it curved out of sight beyond Lambeth Bridge.

A stocky fair-haired man in his late thirties, Steven was employed by the Diamond Syndicate in their Special Operations department. The Diamond Syndicate had its headquarters at No. 2 Manorhouse Street in the City of London, and was the world's largest wholesaler of uncut diamonds. Their Special Operations department functioned as a small undercover group which investigated the theft of uncut diamonds, both internally and in the long supply routes between London and the world's major diamond mines.

Before Steven joined the staff of the Syndicate under Paul Remington in 1979 he had been a detective sergeant with the Metropolitan police. Today he had been invited by a former colleague, Detective Chief Inspector Bryan Raleigh, to a meeting at New Scotland Yard. Although Steven had on several occasions made use of his former connections with the Metropolitan police, he admitted to his boss that he was intrigued by the invitation.

In 1972, Steven Heming and Bryan Raleigh had both joined the Metropolitan police on the same day as probationary constables. When Steven resigned from the force, Detective Sergeant Bryan Raleigh had gone on to take an Open University degree in Fine Arts and was later promoted to detective inspector in the Yard's Art and Antiques Investigation Squad. Two years later he was promoted chief inspector and put in charge of the department.

Steven experienced a pang of nostalgia as he passed the rotating New Scotland Yard sign which featured in so many crime films. He walked into the building's main entrance and reported to the security desk.

'I've an appointment with DCI Raleigh of the Art and Antiques Investigation Squad.'

The plain clothes constable consulted his book. 'Mr Steven Heming?'

'Yes, that's me.' Steven glanced up at the video camera mounted above the security desk. All visitors to the building were captured on video tape, and their image added to the computer logged entry at the end of each day.

The constable pushed a clipboard over the counter. 'Please sign the register and print your name alongside your signature.' He picked up his telephone and punched in a number. 'I have a Mr Steven Heming to see you, sir.' He nodded at Steven. 'You're clear to go up. Take the lift to the fourth floor — DCI Raleigh's office is opposite the lift exit.'

When Steven reached the fourth floor his former colleague was waiting for him at his office door.

Bryan Raleigh held out his hand. 'Great to see you again after all this time — good grief, you still look as fit as ever! Come on in and take a pew.'

Bryan Raleigh was a clear four inches taller than Steven and, with his thin wiry frame, untidy shock of hair and woolly cardigan, looked more like an absent-minded academic than a well-respected detective chief inspector. He waved Steven to a chair, sat down behind his desk and poured out two cups of coffee from a percolator. 'I hate instant coffee, particularly when it comes out of plastic cups from one of those damned automatic machines.'

Steven grinned. 'You always were a rebel.' He glanced around the office. 'This is quite a pleasant niche you have here — perhaps I should have followed your example and specialised.'

'Well, someone has to tangle with these art thieves. I hear you've got a cushy number with the Syndicate.'

'It pays the rent — but tell me, Bryan, what am I doing here, aside from renewing an old acquaintance?'

'Cast your mind back to 1980 — do you remember that audacious theft of the Golconda d'Or diamond in Sydney?'

'Yes, you asked me to have some checks done on the yellow glass replica the gang used.'

Bryan nodded. 'Your gemmologist's report gave us the refractive index, specific gravity and absorption spectra of the glass. But there was nothing in the figures that gave us any clue to a possible source of manufacture — it could have come from any one of hundreds of glass works.'

'Yes, I remember you were pretty frustrated at the time. As far as I'm aware, the Golconda was never recovered.'

'That's right, but recently a new analysis technique has been developed by a company in the Cambridge science park. Using the technique it's possible to identify minute trace elements in glass and produce what could be called a "fingerprint" of that material. We've also just received a report indicating a high ranking Russian might have been responsible for planning the Golconda robbery. The Sydney police still had the glass replica of the Golconda in their crime museum, so we asked them to airmail it to us. When it arrived we sent it to the Cambridge company for testing. When they compared the results of the test with those they had recorded from hundreds of other glass samples, they found it was identical to material coming from a glass factory in Odessa. And — this is the interesting bit — the Russian factory specialises in gemstone replicas.'

'I get your drift Bryan, but how does that get you any closer to finding out who was behind the Golconda affair?'

'I'm coming to that. The report we received about the high-ranking Russian came via Interpol from the Diamond and Gold branch of the South African police. After the breakup of the USSR into a confederation of independent states, several of the top Russians decided to take their chances in the West. The SA report states that Colonel Leo Vessovski, former head of the KGB, is now living in Cape Town and has changed his name to Vandam. He has set himself up as an art dealer, but they suspect that he may be acting as a fence for stolen works of art, and may even be masterminding thefts.'

'So you have one positive link to a glass factory in the former USSR, and a very speculative Vessovski connection — I think you're going to need a bit more than that.'

Bryan Raleigh got up and gazed thoughtfully out of his window at the rush hour traffic streaming over Westminster Bridge. 'It reminded me of the brushes you and your boss Paul Remington had with some of Leo Vessovski's SMERSH operatives in Bangkok.'

'Right — that was when the Ruskies were trying to discredit the Diamond Syndicate and take over its customers. When we proved those fake Chinese diamonds were being mass produced in Moscow, the diplomatic shit really hit the fan. But what of it?'

Bryan Raleigh began pacing the office. 'A witness at the Golconda robbery said she thought one of the gang had a Polish accent. Well, Polish and Russian are not dissimilar. It could be that back in 1980 Colonel Leo Vessovski was already running his own fund-raising organisation outside the USSR — such an enterprise would have had SMERSH operatives on tap in key centres around the world. It would be intriguing if the men in the Sydney gang were identified as SMERSH operatives.'

'That's a bit of a long shot.'

'Perhaps so.' Bryan Raleigh moved across to a filing cabinet and pulled out some papers. 'Take a gander at these two photofit pictures the Sydney police sent us in 1980 — do you recognise either of these men?'

Steven looked carefully at both pictures and shook his head. 'Sorry — the Bangkok affair was a long time ago, and I can't say either of these mugs is familiar.' He hesitated for a moment. 'Can you give me prints of these. I'd like my boss Paul to take a look at them — he tangled with some of Leo Vessovski's operatives in Peking.'

Brian slotted the pictures into his photocopier and handed the duplicates to Steven. He turned his computer monitor round so that they could both view the screen. 'As you know, my department is kept busy logging and tracing stolen works of art.'

He typed in a code on the terminal's keyboard, and a full

colour reproduction of the 'The Scream' by Edvard Munch appeared on the display. 'This computer program has been a great help to us. Apart from showing a picture of the painting, which can be enlarged to show details, it also provides us with a set of basic facts.' Brian accessed a page of data on the monitor. 'This painting, for example, is on show in the National Gallery of Oslo. It's one of the world's best known impressionist paintings and is valued at forty-eight million pounds. Nearly all of the more important paintings and other antiques and works of art can now be displayed in full colour from a central database. In the event of a stolen work of art being recovered, we can quickly identify the article and return it to the owner. We also have access to pictures and details of high value jewellery and unmounted stones.' He keyed in another code and a picture of a golden yellow emerald-cut diamond appeared on the screen.

'Steven leaned forward. 'That's the Golconda d'Or.'

'Correct, but as you can see from the text it still hasn't been recovered. It would be rather neat if we could pin this one down to our friend Leo Vessovski alias Vandam. He's sitting sunning himself in Cape Town, and so far we've nothing concrete on him.'

Steven got up and stretched. 'Well, thanks for bringing me up to date. I'll show the mug shots to Paul and get back to you. We've both got a score to settle with friend Leo. He covered his tracks well over the Peking Diamonds affair, but now he's out of Russia and running his own private show we may be able to find a chink in his armour.'

* * *

When Steven Heming returned to the Diamond Syndicate's offices in 2 Manorhouse Street he found Paul Remington dictating a letter to his secretary. Paul was in his mid-forties, tall and bronzed with close-cropped dark brown hair. Before he joined the Diamond Syndicate and set up their Special Operations Department he had been a commissioned officer in the SAS. He had often used this training in tight corners when dealing with the diamond underworld. Paul Remington paused in his dictation and glanced up at Steven. 'Is it urgent?'

Steven shrugged. 'Not really — but it sure is interesting.'

Paul sighed and nodded to his secretary. 'OK Debbie, it's getting late — we'll finish the report tomorrow.' He turned to Steven. 'How did the mysterious meeting go?'

'The Yard think they've got something on the former head of the KGB, Colonel Leo Vessovski — he's now in Cape Town posing as an art dealer and using the name Vandam.'

'That's interesting, but how does it affect us?'

'Bryan Raleigh gave me copies of the photofit pictures of the two men in the 1980 Golconda d'Or robbery in Sydney. He thinks they may have been two of Leo's men. I thought you should take a look at them.' Steven handed the two photocopies to Paul.

Paul looked at the first one and shook his head. He studied the second one for a few seconds and then looked up at Steven in surprise. 'This is the Russian KGB gorilla who nearly killed me in Peking,' he exclaimed.

Steven grinned. 'Great. It was a long shot, but I had a hunch you might just recognise one of them.'

'If the two men in the Golconda robbery were SMERSH operatives, it's probable that Leo was running them.' Paul paused and looked at the photocopies again. 'These characters could never have planned such a smooth operation by themselves, and it would have needed someone with Leo's level of authority to make it happen.'

Steven nodded. 'Just what I was thinking — and if Leo used his men for extra mural operations back in 1980, he could now be controlling similar activities from Cape Town. I'll phone Bryan with the news — it should earn us a few brownie points at the Yard.'

CHAPTER 3

CAPE TOWN
Saturday 9 October, 1993

Even at the height of apartheid, Cape Town prided itself on its liberalism. Long before colour discrimination was abolished in South Africa, the Nico Malan Opera House, built on the reclaimed land of its harbour foreshore, was playing to mixed audiences, and Cape Town's public transport system had already abandoned the 'nie-blankes' rule. Situated beneath the dramatic geological monolith of Table Mountain, and lying at the western end of the famed Garden Route, the city had for many years featured on the tourist map alongside the Kruger National Park and the Big Hole of Kimberley.

In 1981 Leo Vessovski, former head of the KGB, narrowly escaped implication in an unauthorised plot to destabilise the Diamond Syndicate's operations. From that time on he began laying his plans to leave Russia. Long before the breakup of the USSR, and the dissolution of the KGB, he chose Cape Town as the site of his new headquarters. He had managed to salt away substantial amounts of hard currency culled from the money-change black market in the USSR, the illegal export of ikons, and other equally criminal projects he had initiated in the West. With the vast resources of the KGB under his command he had no difficulty in acquiring a new passport in the name of Leo Vandam.

By 1991, officials in the Foreign Exchange department of the Reserve Bank of South Africa were impatiently awaiting the inflow of foreign investment following Nelson Mandela's release from Robben Island and the country's slow move towards a coalition government. They had welcomed Leo's injection of funds into South Africa, and a residence permit was issued to him in the name of Leo Vandam. The South African police, however, were less impressed and opened a file on the wealthy immigrant from Russia.

Embracing his newly adopted country, Leo Vandam's first move was to purchase a R750,000 property in the exclusive Clifton area, two miles northwest of Table Mountain along the winding coast road to Hout Bay. The two-storey white-walled building was perched at the top of an almost sheer rock face eighty feet above the narrow seafront road. Palm trees grew tenaciously at each side of the house, their roots anchored firmly in crevices that went deep into the rock. The house had a broad paved terrace giving views over the bay. From here, the top station of the Table Mountain cableway was just visible at the western end of the escarpment as it merged into the peaks of the Twelve Apostles behind Camps Bay. At the road level there was a two-car garage which had been blasted out of the rock face.

The only access to the house was by means of a four-person lift cabin which ran almost vertically on a narrow-gauge track up the steep rock face from the side of the garage to the terrace. Visitors had to use a video entry phone to gain access to the cabin which was then pulled up the track by two steel cables reeled in by an electric winch operated from a control point in the house. Leo had been well pleased with the security features of his new property, and had added a few of his own. Remembering a certain notorious establishment at Ober Salzburg in Germany, he named the house 'Eagles Nest'.

On this particular afternoon in October 1993, three men were sitting around a white glass-topped table on the terrace drinking chilled Paarl Chardonnay and enjoying the early spring sunshine. At one end of the table, Leo Vandam sat under a large blue and white umbrella sipping his wine and staring impassively at the shipping scattered thinly across the blue expanse of the bay. He was wearing white shorts and a red cotton T-shirt, neither of which enhanced his corpulent over-indulged body or deflected attention from his almost gross baldness. In former days as Head of the KGB he had retained his army rank of colonel, and had made an impressive figure in a uniform decorated with campaign ribbons. Even dressed casually as he was today he still managed to give the daunting impression of an angry volcano about to erupt.

Sitting next to Leo, his second in command, Clive Drake, nervously pushed his thick-lensed metal frame glasses back over the bridge of his nose and peered short-sightedly at the airmail letter Leo had just handed him. Clive was more austerely dressed than his boss and was wearing baggy grey flannels and a brown safari jacket which only just encompassed his prominent paunch.

Clive Drake had been Security Director of the Coastal Diamond Corporation at Edeldorp on the Namibian coast, and had previously worked in the Diamond and Gold branch of the South African police. In 1978 he had been sentenced to fifteen years imprisonment for his part in an attempt to destroy the workings of a rival diamond mine in the Transvaal. Leo had become aware of Clive after his release from prison earlier in the year. He had made discreet enquiries into his previous organising abilities and, knowing Clive's criminal record would drastically reduce his chances of employment, offered him the post of personal assistant. As he anticipated, Clive jumped at the chance to use his brains again after his stultifying years in prison.

Sitting alongside Clive was a heavily built man wearing sunglasses and blue swimming trunks. His dark crew-cut hair and muscular deeply tanned body were physical attributes markedly different from those of his companions. Oleg Antonovitch, the third member of the team, was once one of Leo's senior operatives in the SMERSH division of the KGB, and now acted as his bodyguard and general assistant. Oleg had willingly joined forces with Leo when he left the USSR for South Africa. At the onset Leo had insisted they conversed only in English, a rule which had initially been a great burden to Oleg who had only acquired a few words of the language during his periods of attachment to various Russian embassies around the world. Now his occasional lapses into Russian only served to irritate Clive Drake, who was by nature suspicious of anything he could not understand.

Clive had finished reading the airmail letter. He looked across at Leo. 'So the painting has arrived safely with our client in the Seychelles,' he commented, and passed the letter to Oleg.

Leo poured himself some more wine. 'On Monday you must check that the money has been transferred to our business account. Have there been any more news items on the Rijksmuseum burglary in the international press?'

Clive shook his head. 'Nothing — not even in the Dutch papers. There's nothing new on the Internet either. I've been in touch with my informant in the South African police, but there have been no more references to the theft on the Interpol network.'

'Good, I think we can mark up another successful business deal — congratulations again on your operational plan, it worked like a well-oiled machine.'

Clive's eyes glinted in appreciation behind his thick glasses. Praise from Leo was rare. He picked up his glass and held it out for the proffered refill. 'Have we had any e-mail response yet to our quotation on the Brazilian order?'

Leo glanced inquiringly at Oleg. 'That was your baby.'

Oleg removed his sunglasses. 'Nothing yet, but as you say in the West, it's early days.' Oleg was pleased with his growing command of the English language. 'However, I think I am near filling in one more piece of operational jigsaw. Our UK contact left a message on the computer. He is faxing us a job advertisement appearing yesterday in Evening Standard. This should give us man on inside.'

Leo nodded approvingly. 'Excellent. Now that Clive has completed his Seychelles assignment I suggest the two of you join forces on this one. I've been able to track down a suitable source of large CZ crystals in Moscow, and we should be getting two samples of the required size in the post. When we hear from Brazil, I'll arrange a visit to Senor Perez in Rio to discuss the final details. With any luck, and if he agrees to our price, we should all get comfortably rich on this one.'

Oleg got up and handed the airmail letter back to Leo. 'I am happy to work with Clive, but would like to be in the action this time. I am getting mouldy sitting around here.'

Leo laughed. 'I think you mean "stale". Now listen to me carefully — that damned Australian photofit picture of you was far too accurate for my peace of mind. It's probably still on Interpol's file, and will continue to make it unsafe for you to operate in the field, particularly in Australia. I'm equally against you operating in the UK. The hornet's nest we will stir up there could bring you up against Paul Remington, and he would certainly recognise you. Clive is unknown in the UK, so it will be his task to set up the team there.'

Oleg looked dejected. 'I would like chance of meeting Paul Remington again. He would not be so lucky as that time in Peking, Colonel.'

Leo's face darkened. He reached up and grabbed Oleg's arm in a vice like grip. 'I've told you before not to address me as colonel. And don't be a fool — never under-estimate the opposition. Those two men in the Syndicate's Special Operations section caused me enough trouble in Russia. I don't want them interfering in my plans again.'

He relaxed his grip on Oleg's arm. 'Be patient — there will be plenty of excitement for you here in South Africa before I've done.' He stood up and smiled grimly. 'This next coup is going to be the biggest one we've attempted. Just make sure the scenario for London is watertight — I want a complete run through with both of you before I go to Rio.'

CHAPTER 4

LONDON
Monday 25 October, 1993

The office used by the Keeper of the Jewel House at the Tower of London was a large but sparsely furnished room in the Beauchamp Tower. At the far side of the room, twin windows looked out through trees across a carefully tended lawn to the sunlit facade of the White Tower. Inside the room the heavy mahogany furniture and the dark drapes framing the windows seemed to mirror the gloomy history of the fortress-prison where three Queens of England were once executed. Although the day was mild, the room felt chilly and the head warden who was sitting alongside the Keeper and Resident Governor of the Tower, General Sir John Battersby, shivered involuntarily.

'Do you mind if I switch on your convector heater, sir?'

'No, of course not, man — should have thought of that myself. Damned place takes ages to warm up on a Monday morning.' Sir John shuffled through the papers on his desk. 'Now we've got down to the final short list, this session shouldn't take too long.'

'That's right, sir. In my opinion there's only one man left on the list who really fits the bill.'

Sir John nodded. 'I agree, but we've still got to go through the motions.'

The advertisement for the post of Jewel House Warden appeared in the Evening Standard on October 7, and had produced eighty-six applicants. After two weeks of interviews this number had been reduced to fifteen, and then to five. Today, the five short-listed applicants had been called back again for a final vetting.

Sir John signalled to the Yeoman warder guarding the door. 'Right, send in Mr Croft.'

As the first of the interviews got under way, the remaining

four applicants sitting in the outer room talked nervously together in hushed tones. They had all satisfied the basic requirements of the advertisement. Their ages ranged between the specified limits of twenty-one and fifty-five, and they all had previous experience in security work, or had served in the HM forces or in the police. The advertisement had also taken pains to make clear, in bold type, the following message:

> Historic Royal Palaces is an equal opportunities employer and welcomes applications from all people regardless of race, sex, marital status or disability.'

Despite this magnanimous sentiment, both the keeper of the Jewel House and his head warden had been secretly relieved to see that all of the applicants were turbanless, male and able.

By midday the last of the five men, a Mr George Freeman, was being interviewed by Sir John and the head warden.

'I'm sorry to put you through yet another interrogation, but as you and the four other applicants have survived two previous interviews, my colleague the head warden and I now have the difficult task of making our final selection.' Sir John looked up and smiled at the middle-aged man sitting in front of his desk. 'Now, Mr Freeman, I see from your application form that you retired from the City of London police two years ago at the age of forty five having reached the rank of sergeant. You've previously told us of your career in the police, and we've seen the excellent character references from your superiors in the force. I'd appreciate it if you would now expand a little more on your activities during the last two years.'

George Freeman squared his shoulders and leaned forward slightly in his chair. 'Well, sir, if you remember, 1991 was the beginning of the recession. I spent the first six months looking round for a job as a security officer. Several of my colleagues who retired a few years earlier supplemented their pensions in this way.'

'Presumably the recession made it difficult for you to find employment of this type?' asked the head warden.

'If I had been prepared to move north, there was a possible job in Liverpool. I'm not married, but my brother and sister are, and both have children. I didn't want to move away from them or my friends. I was born in London, and I still think it's the centre of the civilised world.'

Sir John smiled. 'Well I can't disagree with that sentiment. So what did you do?'

George Freeman settled back in his chair and shrugged his shoulders. 'Where I live in Bromley, there had been a series of house break-ins, mainly at night when people were watching television. 'With no prospect of a job in security, I decided to organise a neighbourhood watch scheme. Although there was no salary, at least I felt I was using the skills I had acquired during my time in the police force. There are now around twenty members of our community who share a rota system of patrols during the evening hours, and I'm pleased to say break-ins have been drastically reduced as a result.'

Sir John nodded approvingly. 'That's a very laudable endeavour. Now, if we offer you the post of Jewel House warden, how do you feel about the job. It entails, as you know, both guarding the Crown Jewels and supervising the flow of visitors through the Jewel House. Would you be comfortable with that?'

'Just try me, sir. I'd regard it as a privilege to guard the royal regalia.' George Freeman's eyes twinkled, 'and I'm well used to controlling the public.'

'I'm sure you are.' Sir John turned and glanced questioningly at the head warden, who nodded in agreement.

'Well, Mr Freeman, my colleague and I are both satisfied with what we've heard. You will no doubt be relieved to know that we will be sending you a formal contract of employment within the next few days. As I mentioned at your first interview, you will be expected to take up the appointment on Monday the first of November, and there will be a probationary period of six months before we put you on permanent staff. The head warden will arrange to have you measured for your uniform. It's still the traditional black tunic with red revers and cuffs — and of course the black hat with gold braid.'

Sir John stood up and offered him his hand. 'Congratulations, and welcome to the team.'

* * *

That night in his semi-detached house in Bromley, George Freeman settled back comfortably in his armchair and picked up the telephone. He keyed in a number, and waited for a few seconds while the coded digits transmitted the call through the exchange in Cape Town. He heard the ringing tones and then a familiar voice came on the line. 'Vandam antiques.'

'Hallo, is that Clive Drake? It's George Freeman here — I've got the job.' He paused for a moment as Clive plied him with questions. 'No, they took the sob-story hook, line and sinker. Thanks for the script. At least my police credentials were genuine, so there was no problem there. I start next Monday — there's a bit of a hustle on because of the work on the new Jewel House. As soon as I hear the date of the move to the new site I'll be in touch. It should be sometime in the New Year. In the meanwhile, don't forget I need that money by the end of the week — the bookmakers are getting ugly.'

CHAPTER 5

RIO DE JANEIRO
Tuesday 23 November, 1993

It has been said that Rio has only two seasons, summer and hot weather. While this may be a slight exaggeration, the sun-drenched climate of its famous Copacabana beach certainly lasts all year long, rising to a tropical peak in February. However, in November, the month that marks the beginning of the long carnival season, the temperature is more moderate. Even so, Leo Vandam was glad he had arranged an early morning appointment for the meeting that day with his multi-millionaire client Senor Roman Perez. When Perez was a young graduate mineralogist fresh out of university, the foundation of his present wealth began in 1952 with his discovery of a small, but important, gold mine high up in the mountain range to the north-west of Rio.

Several years later he sold his shares in the mine and invested the money in land development projects around the growing residential areas of Rio. He became interested in local politics, associated with all the right people, and joined the Yacht Club. There he was introduced to a beautiful young socialite, and after a lightning courtship they were married the following spring. Sadly, two years later his wife died while giving birth to their son, Juan. As a dutiful father, Perez made sure in the intervening years that his son had the best of everything money could buy. By the age of twenty-five Juan, now a handsome young man, had degenerated into a compulsive gambler, a womaniser and a wastrel.

His participation in the city's riotous nightlife often brought him to the attention of the police and was a constant source of dismay and irritation to his father. During an evening of social drinking on Leo Vandam's last visit to Rio, Roman Perez had taken him into his confidence and spoken of his son's escapades. Although Leo's own wife died many years ago during the siege of Leningrad, and he had no children of his own, he felt sorry for Perez.

When Leo arrived in Brazil the previous morning, Roman Perez had telephoned him from his palatial home in the mountains at Teresopolis, sixty miles north of Rio. It seemed Perez had recently become aware that his home was under surveillance. He had therefore suggested that instead of Leo visiting Teresopolis as on other occasions, they choose a less conspicuous rendezvous where they could mingle with the crowds.

Following instructions, Leo took a taxi from his hotel on Copacabana beach to Cosme Velho Square. From there he caught a small single-carriage train which wound its way through the Tijuca National Park forest before climbing slowly up the north west side of the 2,400 foot high Corcovado Peak.

When the train reached the terminus just beneath the summit, Leo got out and strolled up the steep pathway to the massive granite statue of Christ the Redeemer which dominated one end of the long balustraded viewing platform. He walked round the base of the statue, threading his way through groups of tourists, and then descended a flight of granite steps to the far end of the platform. From this vantage point he could see all of Rio spread out beneath him. In the middle distance was Sugar Loaf mountain and beyond that the broad sweep of Guanabara Bay.

Leo turned around and looked up at the statue. From the number of cameras in action around him this was clearly the best point from which to photograph it. The Christ figure stood facing Sugar Loaf mountain and the Bay to the north-east. Its arms were spread wide, and its head, now half in shadow, was tilted slightly downwards as if looking at the city and its people. Leo smiled to himself as he remembered hearing of an inhabitant of neighbouring Sao Paulo who insisted that Christ was in fact raising his hands in despair at the fun-loving and dissipated life style of the people of Rio de Janeiro.

He was just about to retrace his steps when he saw a grey-haired elderly man walking towards him dressed in a fawn-coloured lightweight suit, white open-neck shirt, and a red cravat.

'Good morning, Leo,' said the man, doffing his white sombrero, 'and, once again, welcome to Rio.' Roman Perez shook Leo warmly by the hand. 'Thank you for agreeing to this rather elevated rendezvous. As I mentioned on the telephone, I have become aware of late that my movements are being watched.'

Leo took Perez's elbow and led him to the balustrade overlooking Rio. 'Don't look now, but there's a dark-haired young man standing watching us at the top of the steps.'

Perez laughed. 'Relax, that's my minder — he'll make sure we're not disturbed. Now tell me, how are your plans going?'

'We've just heard the royal regalia is being moved to the new site on Sunday, February 6. Our man is in position, and Clive Drake has recruited the London team and arranged the transport. If all goes according to plan, and we allow a few weeks for all the fuss to die down, the stone should be in your hands by the end of February.'

Perez's eyes glinted. 'Excellent, my friend. The acquisition of the world's most famous diamond will add the finishing touch to my private collection. Between us we will have accomplished the impossible — and the joke is no-one will even suspect.'

Leo massaged his bald dome. The morning sun was beginning to make itself felt, and he made a mental note to buy a hat. 'This will have been our most complicated and expensive operation to date. I trust you will not take offence if I remind you of our business arrangement.'

Perez frowned. 'Such a reminder is not necessary between partners in crime.' He took an envelope from his breast pocket. 'This contains half of your fee as agreed — a certified banker's draft for two million US dollars. The other half will be paid when the diamond is securely in my safe at Teresopolis.'

Leo pocketed the envelope without opening it. 'At just over seven and a half thousand dollars per carat, I think you will have a bargain there — but won't the stone make the Golconda look rather insignificant?'

Roman Perez chuckled. 'I like your humour, Leo. However, I may not keep the big diamond for ever. The only thing I have coveted more than this diamond is an English Knighthood. Now let me reveal to you my hidden agenda. Queen Elizabeth is not getting any younger, and some time in the not too distant future there is bound to be another coronation ceremony in the UK. Just suppose I was instrumental in finding a key item in the coronation regalia and returning it to a grateful monarch — do you not think I would then be in line for a knighthood?'

Leo stared at Perez in astonishment. 'You sly old rogue. So that's what this is really all about.'

'To be known as Sir Perez in our society would mean a lot. The idea has long appealed to me.'

Leo wiped the perspiration from his bald head. 'But surely in the UK there are ways of buying a knighthood at much less than the fee you are paying me.'

'Maybe, but doing it this way is more certain — and I get to enjoy the company of the big stone for a few years as a bonus.'

Roman Perez linked arms with Leo. 'Now, my old friend, let us go back down this mountain before I get nose bleed.'

As they strolled back to the base of the statue, Perez pointed out the dark red lustrous grains visible in the granite steps. 'Would you believe it — those bits of red are all garnets.'

'I can believe anything of Rio,' confessed Leo. 'Tell me, Roman, how is your son. Is he still causing you problems?'

'I continue to settle his gambling debts,' sighed Perez. 'The only time I see him is when he wants money.' When they reached the car park at the bottom of the pathway, Perez hailed a waiting taxi. 'First, we must have lunch to celebrate the completion of the first part of our business deal. Then, I will take you to one of the beach bars where you can enjoy a good steak and sample our draught beer. Finally, to end the day, we will take in one of the noitadas de samba — a samba night show. The mulatto dancing girls who perform in these shows belong to the many samba academies in Rio. They make their own exotic costumes and rehearse all year for the carnival. Tonight I can guarantee they will make us both feel young again!'

CHAPTER 6

LONDON
Monday 24 January, 1994

A hard overnight frost had encrusted the lawns at the Tower of London with fine white ice crystals, much to the displeasure of the ravens who regarded these open spaces as their own particular territory. There had been ravens living at the Tower long before Charles II decreed that six of the birds should be kept there permanently, a decree influenced by the legend that if the ravens disappear, the Tower will fall.

An hour before the Jewel House opened to the public, the head warden called a meeting of his staff in the east wing of the old Waterloo Barracks Block. The new Jewel House had been designed to use the entire ground floor of that wing, and work on the display areas was almost completed. A series of Victorian-style cases had already been installed in the much larger space now available, and these were being made ready to take the treasures of the crown jewels and the royal regalia when they were finally transferred from their present site in the west wing. The planning of the new layout and preparations for the transfer of the priceless jewels and regalia had taken well over a year, and during that time both the existing Jewel House and the design of the new site had been the subjects of much criticism.

'We're expecting a throughput of around fifteen thousand people a day when this section is opened, so you can see why these two moving walkways have been installed on each side of the crown jewels display cases — but don't worry, the travelators are not made of bouncy rubber as someone claimed, and they'll be running much slower than those at London airport.' The head warden acknowledged the ripple of laughter from his group of wardens. 'In fact the travelators will only be run at peak times, so I don't know what all the fuss was about.'

'As you know, we've already been informed that the old Jewel House will be closed after Sunday January 30. This will give the crown jewellers plenty of time to check out and clean the various items in the collection before the transfer. While this is going on you'll be split up into two groups. One group will remain in the old Jewel House and assist in the removal of the items one by one for cleaning by the jewellery experts. Members of the other group will report to the new Jewel House, where they will roll up their sleeves and help in the cleaning of the new display cabinets. You will not, of course, be wearing your uniforms during this period. I'll also remind you that the keeper and the curator will be looking in from time-to-time, so watch your language. After each item of the royal regalia has been cleaned it will for security reasons be temporarily returned to its old display cabinet until the final Sunday evening. To spread the load, the rest of the collection will be transferred to the new site earlier that week.'

The head warden paused. 'Any questions so far?'

One of the younger members of his team raised a hand. 'Yes, chief, as it's going to be rather a mucky job, particularly in the east wing, are we getting any protective clothing?'

'Rest assured, you'll all be issued with coveralls. But as you'll be moving around the site you must remember to wear your ID cards where they can easily be seen — I don't want any of you being nicked by the extra police patrols which will be on duty up to and during the transfer.' The head warden consulted his paperwork. 'What I'm about to tell you now is top secret, and I don't want you talking about it to anyone, and that means wives, girlfriends, male and female companions, and those who aren't too sure.' At this there were some nudges and knowing winks among his audience.

'First of all, at the end of that week you will be doing a late shift starting at ten o'clock on the night of Sunday February 6 — that's the night the crown jewels will be removed again from their display cases, crated and moved to the new site here in the east wing.'

'We are getting double-time for night work, aren't we, chief,' asked one of the wardens.

The head warden sighed. 'That's already been agreed with the royal palaces' personnel department as you well know, so stop wasting my time on trivialities. Now at precisely ten o'clock that night we will be joined by six armed police from the Yard's anti-terrorist squad. Once they are in position in the old Jewel House and have established communications with their radio van on the south side of the river, I will de-activate the alarm system. You will then start removing the pieces from the display cabinets and packing them into their individual boxes, ready for the transfer. This will take place through the connecting sub-basement tunnel with the six anti-terrorist police providing an armed escort.'

The group of ten wardens appeared suitably impressed with the arrangements, and the head warden completed his briefing with a final caution. 'I have also been instructed to warn you not to be late reporting for duty that night — that is if you want the extra money. From ten o'clock until the job is completed there will be police cars stationed at all the approaches to the Tower.' He eyed the warden who had queried the overtime rates. 'After that time, nobody, and that includes you, will be allowed through.'

* * *

When warden George Freeman returned to his home in Bromley that night he put through a call to Clive Drake in Cape Town. When Clive came on the line he sounded anxious.

'Have you got problems,' he asked guardedly.

'No, relax — everything's fine. After I found out that the armed escort for the transfer was using the Bishopsgate police station, I started having a lunchtime drink in the pub next door. Well, it paid off at last. One of the regulars there is a police van driver. When I told him I was an ex-copper and was working as a warden at the Tower, he got quite pally. Lunchtime today I met him again, and he got talking about the February operation. The good news is I've got the information you wanted.'

'That's first rate,' exclaimed Clive. 'I need those details before I leave for the UK this Friday, so fax them through now.'

'That's not all — I spent Saturday with one of my old colleagues at the Yard — he's in the signals section. We were exchanging a few yarns, and he let slip the radio channels their mobile control van will be using on February 6. As he knows I'm in on the move at the Tower, I guess he thought it was safe to tell me. Anyway, I figured if you had the details you could patch in to their traffic. I'll fax their schedules through to you with the rest of the info.'

'Thanks, George. The way my plans are firming up I may have to jam those channels. I won't be contacting you directly in the UK until the show is over. Oh, and don't forget to wear your ID card on February 6 so my boys can pick you out.'

CHAPTER 7

LONDON
Sunday 6 February, 1994

At nine-fifty in the evening, a dark blue police van pulled slowly out of Bishopsgate Police Station and turned south towards Bank. On board, the six members seconded from the police anti-terrorist squad were in jocular mood at the prospect of a change in their normal routine. All of them wore bullet-proof jackets over their dark blue battledress and were armed with automatic FLN rifles. The sergeant in charge of the squad glanced at his watch.

'We should be passing through the police cordon around Tower Hill just before ten o'clock,' he announced. With a reduction in IRA activity he was glad his team would be providing merely a token security guard that night. Only two of the them had ever had occasion to use the FLN in action and, as an ex-member of the SAS, he was well aware of his men's comparative inexperience.

'Right, lads,' he barked out. 'Now settle down and listen up. Re-check the safety catches on your weapons — I don't want any of you getting excited and firing off a loose round when you're in the Jewel House.'

One of the newest members of the team eased the rifle sling off his shoulder and inspected his weapon. 'Would you rather we unloaded the clips and handed you the rounds, sarg.' He turned and grinned at his companions.

'Now don't give me any lip, boy. You're here on my recommendation, so just keep your nose clean.'

By now the van had arrived at Bank and was turning down King William Street. On a late Sunday evening there was little traffic about. At Monument, the driver turned left into Eastcheap. Halfway down the road he slowed the van and then stopped. Ahead, a large articulated lorry had jack-knifed across the road. The driver of the lorry was standing dejectedly at the side of his cab scratching his head. The police van driver cursed silently to himself. He picked up his handset and pressed the button.

'Zero base, this is Zero one in Eastcheap. There's a jack-knifed lorry blocking the road so I'm diverting down Lovat Lane into Lower Thames Street. Zero one, out.'

'Roger, Zero one. Zero base, out.' The operator in the radio control van stationed on the other side of the Thames moved the magnetic marker on his map in confirmation of the diversion. A few seconds later a sustained burst of static-like interference cut communications for several minutes between the police van and the radio control van. When it cleared, the driver of the police car stationed at the west end of Tower Hill came on the air.

'Zero base, this is Zero two. I have visual contact with Zero one leaving Lower Thames Street. Zero two, out.'

The radio control van was positioned on the riverside terrace near London Bridge. From here the operator had a clear view across the river to the Tower and could see the headlights of the police van as it swung into Tower Hill. 'Acknowledged, Zero two. I have a visual also. Zero base, out.' He leaned across to his map and moved the magnetic marker onto the Tower of London.

The man in charge of the armed squad in the dark blue van turned to his team. 'Right, smarten yourselves up lads, and pick up your equipment — we're just about to enter the grounds of the Tower. When the van stops I want you out at the double and lined up at the side entrance to Waterloo Barracks block as rehearsed.'

The van entered the gateway at the bottom of Tower Hill, and followed the cobbled road as it curved left along the river frontage of the Tower. The driver swung in over the moat bridge near the end of the road and paused briefly to wave at the two armed police guarding the entrance to the Tower. Then he drove under the Queen Elizabeth arch and up the incline past the White Tower until he reached the west corner of Wellington Barracks. Under the critical gaze of the sergeant, the squad shouldered their automatic rifles and disembarked. The van driver struggled down from his cab with a metal equipment case in each hand and followed the men down the side of the building. The curator was waiting for the anti-terrorist squad at the side entrance to the barracks. The sergeant held up his police ID card and saluted.

'You're bang on schedule,' commented the curator looking at his watch. He unlocked the massive outer door and ushered the group inside. When they were all assembled in the short entrance corridor he closed and bolted the outer door and led them down into the bunker-like area of the Jewel House.

Inside the Jewel House, only the royal regalia remained to be packed and transported to the new site. Sir John Battersby, Keeper and Resident Governor of the Tower, was leaning nonchalantly on the handrail encircling the lower viewing level and talking to the head warden. The group of ten wardens were wearing grey coveralls and sitting in relaxed attitudes around the lower level, seemingly oblivious of the priceless array of jewels only a few inches away behind the armour-plate glass panels of the star-shaped central display unit.

One of the young wardens turned to his companion George Freeman. 'I see the police squad are carrying respirator bags — what's that all about?'

George grinned. 'I expect they heard you had curry for supper tonight.'

The sergeant in charge of the squad began stationing his men strategically around the perimeter of the room. Under the watchful eye of the curator, the van driver was busy placing one of the heavy metal cases at each side of the upper display area. As he laid each case down on the floor he snapped open its lid and flipped a switch.

'What are they for?' The driver looked up to find the curator standing beside him.

'They're radio relay units — with all the metal in here we need some extra power to keep our portable sets in touch with the control van on the other side of the river.'

'Do you really need two of them?'

'We always carry a backup unit.' The curator sniffed and

walked across to where the keeper and the head warden were standing.

The sergeant, satisfied that everything was arranged to his satisfaction, joined the keeper and his colleagues. 'Excuse me, Sir John — we're ready when you are.'

Sir John Battersby turned to his head warden and nodded. The warden walked across to a panel set in the wall. He unlocked a door in the panel and took a handset out of the recess.

'Activate the code unit now.' He waited for a confirmation and then replaced the handset. A few seconds later a red lamp started flashing inside the recess. The head warden keyed a code number into the digital pad mounted alongside the handset and closed the door. A few more seconds passed and then the lights inside the central display unit suddenly went out, leaving the room only dimly lit. Almost immediately a set of ceiling lights came on accompanied by three blasts on a klaxon. The warden walked back and leaned over the handrail.

'OK lads, the alarm is deactivated — you can start bringing the major pieces out now just as we rehearsed. Put on your gloves and start with the imperial state crown. When you've done that, bring out the orb, and then the sceptre. I'll call out the rest of the sequence after that.'

Two of the wardens removed the panels at the far side of the display unit and disappeared inside. They re-emerged within the circular access area in the very centre of the star-shaped glass unit and began lifting out the first three items of the royal regalia. Five more wardens formed a human chain to pass the pieces back to a felt covered table in the centre of the upper level. Here, three wardens were waiting ready to pack each piece into in its individually designed box.

The heavy imperial state crown was laid carefully on the table and wrapped in foam rubber before being placed in its box. The next to be packed was the orb. When the royal sceptre arrived at the table, the sergeant handed his rifle to the van driver and walked forward raising his hand for attention.

'Now listen to me everyone,' he shouted, his voice breaking the almost solemn silence that had descended during the removal of the main items of the royal regalia.

The keeper and his staff looked round in surprise at the sergeant. Their next shock came when they saw the armed squad of five men and the van driver were wearing gas masks and had lined up across the room with their rifles at the ready. The bogus sergeant in charge of this menacing group walked forward two paces.

'We are not your friendly anti-terrorist police from Bishopsgate Police Station. Follow my instructions, and no harm will come to you.' He pointed to the two wardens inside the glass display unit. 'Come out you two and join the others. I want all of you facing me on the far side of the handrail'.

When they had all lined up behind the rail, the 'sergeant' singled out two of his men. 'Look after the sceptre — you know what to do.'

The keeper made a determined effort to regain his composure. 'There's no possibility you can succeed in this madness — the whole area is cordoned off by police. Be sensible and put down your guns before someone gets hurt.'

The 'sergeant' smiled at him. 'I like your spirit Sir John.' He pulled a revolver from his belt and aimed it at him. 'As I've already said, no-one will get hurt if they obey my orders. Now — all of you — face down on the floor before I lose my temper.'

When they were all lying down in the walkway surrounding the display unit, the 'sergeant' donned his gas mask and pulled a small control unit from his pocket. He pressed a button on the unit and a cloud of anaesthetising gas flowed out of the cylinders concealed in the two metal cases. Seeing the cloud of gas billowing towards them, some of the wardens tried to struggle up, but the armed group had already moved forward and forced them down again at gun point.

The 'sergeant' waited a few minutes more for the gas to take full effect, then he walked across to the huddled forms of the thirteen men lying unconscious on the floor and prodded them with his boot. Satisfied there was no reaction, he checked the names on the wardens' ID badges until he found George Freeman. By now the ventilation system had cleared away the last traces of the gas, and the 'sergeant' stood up and signalled for his men to remove their gas masks. He bent down again and dragged warden George Freeman halfway out of the lower level and called to the two men working on the sceptre. 'This is the one — slip the package in his inside pocket. The rest of you fall back on me.'

When the four other members of the gang joined him, he glanced at his watch. 'Right lads — time to go. Our transport will be arriving in five minutes'. As he finished speaking there was a deafening explosion and the outer door to the Jewel House was blown off its hinges and landed with a crash at the entrance to the display area accompanied by a cloud of smoke. The sergeant and the rest of the gang threw themselves to the floor as a hail of bullets sprayed across the Jewel House and ricocheted off the walls.

Through the clearing smoke they could see khaki-uniformed figures moving into position in the corridor beyond the entrance. The van driver upended one of the metal cases and, lying prone on the floor behind it, he began returning bursts of automatic gunfire into the haze. The 'sergeant' crawled across to the second case and, using it as a portable shield, moved forward to the two men who were lying under the table isolated from their companions.

'Did you get the package to George Freeman?'

The men gave him the thumbs up sign and then ducked as another hail of bullets swept the room.

'I've had quite enough of this,' grunted the 'sergeant'. In the lull that followed he scrambled up and attempted to grab the sceptre from the table above them, but another burst of gunfire from the entrance corridor pinned him down again beside the two men. Cursing, he rolled over on his back and, using his revolver, carefully shot out the ceiling lights.

'That evens things up a bit,' he gasped in the welcome half light. 'Now, when I shout "let's go", give me covering fire. I'll get the rest of the team out of the back door and up to the roof. When we're clear, get that bloody sceptre off the table. If it gets shot to pieces the boss will use our guts for garters.'

After the next exchange of cross-fire the 'sergeant' crawled back to the rest of his team. Then, raising his voice he shouted, 'let's go,' and while the two men under the table continued to fire short bursts at the entrance, the five of them made a dash for the rear door.

As soon as they were clear, one of the two remaining men grabbed the edge of the felt tablecloth on which the sceptre was resting. He tugged the cloth down sharply and caught the sceptre as it fell. Then he got to his feet and made a run for the door, holding the sceptre in his left hand and his rifle in the other. Halfway to the door there was a burst of gunfire and a bullet hit him in the left wrist. The tendons parted and he screamed in pain as his fingers lost their grip. The sceptre fell to the floor and rolled under the handrail into the lower section of the viewing area.

The remaining man heard the scream, and toppled the table onto its side to give himself some cover. He fired a final burst in the direction of the entrance and then sprinted doubled-up across the room and dragged the wounded man through the rear door. He could see blood spurting from the gaping wound in the man's wrist and quickly bound it up with his handkerchief.

The two men found the bottom of the stairwell that spiralled up to the roof and struggled up four flights of well-worn steps. At the top they joined the 'sergeant' and their other four companions on the landing that led out to the roof. They could hear the crash of army boots on the stairs below, but much more welcome to their ears was the low thudding beat above their heads that was getting louder every second.

'Thank god the transport is on schedule,' panted the 'sergeant'. He flung open the door leading to the flat roof. 'Right, all of you outside — I'll keep the army boys busy until you're on board.' He fired a short burst down into the well of the building. Although it was impossible to see the men who were on the staircase below him, he knew a good percentage of the rounds he fired must have ricocheted around the stone stairwell like a flight of angry bees. In the short lull that followed he clipped his last magazine into the rifle. By now the thudding roar from the roof had reached deafening pitch and a storm force wind was hurling dust and debris at him through the open door to the roof. 'Time to go,' he muttered to himself through clenched teeth. He fired a final burst down into the stairwell and ran out through the doorway to the waiting Chinook helicopter.

* * *

Across the river, the radio controller and his colleagues in the communications van had heard the crash of the explosion as the SAS team blew in the door of the Jewel House, followed by the muffled sounds of sporadic gunfire. Now they were about to see the final act of the drama played out in front of them as a Chinook helicopter flew in low across the Thames and hovered above the old Waterloo Barracks block. A few seconds later the helicopter touched down at the western end of the building's flat roof. They counted six figures running towards the machine's open door. A few seconds later a seventh figure appeared. It turned round and tossed something back into the roof exit. As this last figure scrambled aboard the Chinook, they saw a bright flash from the exit door followed by the dull bang of an explosion.

Then the helicopter took off, gained altitude and swung south across the river. At this point several other figures emerged onto the roof, and they could hear the staccato sound of automatic fire as the SAS pursuit team opened up on the helicopter. When the Chinook was halfway across the river it turned eastwards. Soon it was approaching the London docks and effectively out of range of the SAS weapons which had now stopped firing. Then, to the astonishment of the onlookers there was a blinding flash, and the fast-moving helicopter, just visible against the dark night sky, was transformed into a brilliant fireball which lit up the shoreline of warehouses bordering the London Docks. Seconds later the dull boom of the explosion reached them. As they watched in disbelief, the fireball disintegrated into a multitude of individual burning fragments which fell like spent fireworks into the blackness below. The twin rotors were the last to fall, the blades turning like giant sycamore seeds as they floated slowly down to the river.

* * *

Clive Drake was also watching the dying throes of the big helicopter as he stood at the window of his seventh floor room in the Tower Hotel. He had carefully chosen this site for his London headquarters as the hotel was built on what was once St Katherine's Dock and afforded him an all-round uninterrupted view of the Tower of London and the river. When the last flames of the helicopter wreckage had been quenched by the cold waters of the Thames, Clive took off his thick-lensed glasses and polished them thoughtfully. He collapsed the telescopic aerials on his radio detonator and channel jammer and packed them carefully in his suitcase.

'As they say, dead men tell no tales,' he mused, and turned on the bedside radio to listen to the midnight news bulletin.

CHAPTER 8

LONDON
Monday 7 February, 1994

Details of the attack on the Jewel House in the Tower of London were sketchy in the early morning radio newscasts. By the time Paul Remington and his wife Stephanie were having breakfast with their eleven-year-old son Jason a few more facts were being revealed on BBC2's eight o'clock news.

Stephanie lay her hand on Jason's arm. 'Are you quite sure about the dates for the school visit to France. You know we've booked a holiday in South Africa for March.'

'Of course I'm sure, mum. Don't fuss. The school will be sending you the details.'

Paul held up his hand for silence. 'Just a minute — what's that about the Tower.' He turned up the volume on the kitchen radio.

> '...latest reports indicate that the raid by seven armed men failed when an anonymous telephone call alerted Scotland Yard. An SAS team was immediately dispatched to the Tower, and after an exchange of gun fire regained control of the Jewel House. The armed men then escaped to the roof of Waterloo Barracks, the building which contains the Jewel House. From there they were lifted off by helicopter, which subsequently exploded in mid-air over the Thames. Further details of the raid will be given later this morning by the commissioner of police at a special news conference to be held in New Scotland Yard. Now for the rest of the news ... '

Paul switched off the radio. 'Wow — that sounds like an attempt to steal the crown jewels,' he exclaimed. 'I understand from Steven that all the other valuables in the Jewel House were moved to the new site last week. Something must have gone badly wrong with the security arrangements last night.'

'Doesn't take a PhD to figure out that would be the ideal time have a go at the Crown Jewels,' commented Jason, avoiding his mother's attempt to comb his unruly mop of auburn hair. He grabbed a piece of buttered toast from Paul's plate and got up from the table. 'Must rush, we've got gym for the first two periods.'

Jason went to a private school in a college at Clarence Gate on the south side of Regents Park, and was able to walk through the Park to school each day from his parent's third floor flat in Prince Albert Road.

When Jason had gone Paul sighed. 'I hope we made the right choice with that school. They seem to spend a lot of time on physical activities.'

'Well, there wasn't much choice around here four years ago, and it does mean he can get there and back on his own — I'm still a working girl, remember.' Stephanie cleared up the breakfast things and put the mugs and plates in the dishwasher.

Paul and Stephanie first met in the Diamond Syndicate's offices at 2 Manorhouse Street in the City of London sixteen years ago. She was working as secretary to Sir James Crichton, the Syndicate's Chairman, and Paul had just been engaged to set up the company's Special Operations department. They had immediately been attracted to each other, and Paul began dating the vivacious redhead. Within a few weeks Stephanie had thrown caution to the winds and moved into Paul's flat on the north side of Regent's park. They were married in the autumn of 1981 and Jason was born the following summer, the auburn hair on his baby head a compromise between his father's brown curly locks and his mother's red tresses. Now a lively young schoolboy, Jason's passions at the moment were divided equally between sport and science, and he was having difficulty in deciding whether he wanted to become a Wimbledon tennis champion or an astronaut.

When Paul and Stephanie left the flat and drove to work through the drizzle of a grey February morning little did they realise that five years later they and their son Jason would find themselves in South Africa caught up in a dangerous sequel to the Tower of London raid.

* * *

In New Scotland Yard, DCI Bryan Raleigh and his colleagues in the Art and Antiques Investigation Squad were gathered round a television set in his office to watch the broadcast of the commissioner's news conference. At half past eleven, the BBC interrupted their programmes with the announcement of a special news item in which the Commissioner of Police, Sir Noel Lancaster, would make a statement concerning an attempted raid on the Tower of London. A few seconds later the picture on the screen showed the rotating triangular sign of New Scotland Yard.

'I wish I had a fiver for every time that's appeared on television,' sighed Bryan, easing his long wiry frame into the unyielding steel and plastic chair.

The picture of the rotating sign faded and was replaced by a view of the craggy featured grey-haired commissioner seated behind his desk.

'Some of you may have been aware of the long term plans to replace the Jewel House at the Tower of London with a more modern and secure one. These plans were due to come to fruition in a few days time after the many invaluable artifacts, including the crown jewels, had been transferred to a new Jewel House in the east wing of the Waterloo Barracks.'

The picture cut to a side view of the commissioner, and then panned left to show several rows of seated journalists, and behind them a group of photographers and a television camera team. The picture changed again to a head and shoulders view of the commissioner.

'Last night, during the final phase of the transfer, and while the crown jewels were being removed from their display case, a gang of armed men entered the Jewel House.' He paused and took a deep breath. 'At the time, the resident governor of the Tower, the curator, and the head warden with his team of ten attendants were all in the Jewel House, and were forced at gunpoint to lie on the floor.'

The commissioner paused again and took a sip of water.

'A few minutes after the raid began, an anonymous telephone call was made to these offices warning us that a gang of armed men had broken into the Jewel House. An SAS team was immediately alerted and sent to the Tower. There they managed to break into the locked and barred Jewel House and to beat off the armed gang, who retreated and escaped onto the roof of the Waterloo Barracks. A helicopter then landed on the roof of the barracks, rescued the armed gang and took off again. The SAS opened fire on the machine and brought it down in the Thames near the London Docks. Early this morning nine bodies were recovered from the river by the Thames River Police, and further salvage work is being done to recover the wreckage of the helicopter. No-one among those present in the Jewel House was injured by the armed gang or during the subsequent exchanges of gunfire between the gang and the SAS. The crown jewels are being examined by experts at the moment, but so far there are no indications that anything is damaged or missing.'

The commissioner looked across at the group of newsmen. 'That is all I can tell you at the moment, but if you have any questions I will attempt to answer them to the best of my ability.'

A journalist in the front row raised his hand. 'John Drifield, Evening News. Sir Noel, is there any possibility that this was the work of the IRA?'

'As far as we know, the para-military wing of Sinn Fein was not involved on this occasion, but of course there is always the possibility that this was the work of another terrorist group such as the Irish National Liberation Army. As this seems to have been a failed attempt at a robbery, and as there are no survivors of the gang, we may never know the answer to that question.'

A hand shot up from the middle of the second row. 'James Cross, Daily Mail. Can you tell us what security precautions, or, more to the point, what physical protection was being given to both the people in the Jewel House and in particular to the nation's crown jewels during this transfer operation?'

A murmur of approval rose from the assembled journalists at

this line of questioning. The subject of security and the apparent lack of it was clearly uppermost in everyone's mind.

'I'm afraid I cannot give you any details of the security arrangements in force last night for obvious reasons, but I can assure you they were considered adequate and appropriate.'

Another hand shot up. 'Robert Lasenby, Daily Telegraph. I think we can infer from what happened last night that those security arrangements fell well short of what could be considered "adequate and appropriate".'

The commissioner scowled at the man. 'You can infer what you like. Until we have been able to question everyone who was in the Jewel House last night, and to build up a complete picture of the events which took place, I will not be able to make any further comments on our security arrangements.'

A girl in the back row stood up. 'Julia Martin, Daily Express. Sir Noel, will the events which happened at the Tower last night delay the Queen's opening of the new Jewel House next month?'

The Commissioner forced a smile at the young lady. 'There is still some work to be completed in the new Jewel house — for instance the video projection units have yet to be installed. The Crown Jewels will also need to be carefully checked for any damage sustained in the raid before they can be placed on display. In view of these factors, we have already agreed with the Queen to postpone the formal opening ceremony until March 24. Thank you, ladies and gentlemen — that is all.'

Bryan Raleigh leaned forward and switched off the television set. 'That was a masterly job of omission. If he'd admitted that the anti-terrorist squad sent to protect the Crown Jewels was highjacked only a few hundred yards from the Tower, there'd have been a riot.'

One of Bryan's colleagues looked surprised. 'I've only just come on duty — what's the story about that?'

Bryan got up and helped himself to coffee from his percolator. 'Apparently, a jack-knifed lorry blocked the path of the police van carrying the anti-terrorist squad, and they diverted out of Eastcheap into Lovat Lane. Halfway down the lane an identical police van blocked their way, and before they could back up someone punched a hole through the side of the van and pumped in anaesthetising gas. At the same time a steel rope was lashed around the van to prevent the doors from being opened.'

'What about their radio, they must have had time to get a call out.'

'Mysteriously, a burst of static interference blocked all communication on the channels they were using. The jack-knifed van disappeared without trace, but at least we've got the van the gang abandoned at the Tower. That's not the end of it — there are two other mysteries. Number one, the phone call telling the Yard about the attack on the Tower — the duty officer who took the call swears the man who spoke to him had a South African accent. Number two, the exploding helicopter. The SAS officer in charge of the rescue team said it was unlikely to have been shot down by them as the machine had been out of range of their weapons for several minutes before it blew up.'

'Have we got anything on the helicopter yet?'

'Yes, but even that is a dead end. It was identified as a Chinook helicopter and was hired at Stansted airport by two men using false papers. They paid cash in advance, left a certified banker's draft as deposit and then filed a flight plan to the Hook of Holland. After the machine took off, our man at Stansted says it was tracked by radar as it flew south-east to the Thames estuary. Then it simply disappeared from the radar screen. At that point he thinks it may have dropped to a low altitude and then turned due west and followed the river until it came to the Tower.'

Bryan stretched his lanky frame and ruffled his hair. In his loose-fitting woolly cardigan he could easily have been mistaken for an eccentric professor. 'The main thing that puzzles me is the exploding helicopter. If the explosion wasn't caused by gunfire, and the Chinook seems to have been well out of range of the SAS when it blew up, then there must have been a bomb on board. It looks to me as if the mastermind behind the raid might just have included a bomb in his scheme for insurance purposes. If the raid failed, as it did, this would have been an ideal way to destroy any evidence by killing off all the participants. But a bomb could only be activated once it was known that the raid was a failure. Ergo, the bomb must have been exploded remotely by someone on the ground who was in radio contact with the gang.'

'I follow your reasoning, but what do you think will happen now,' asked the youngest member of the Art and Antiques Investigation Squad.

'There'll be an inquiry of course. It's clear there's been a serious leak of the security arrangements, but with no apparent harm done to the crown jewels, and only a few cases of damaged ego, the whole episode will probably fade into history alongside the gunpowder plot.'

Five years later, DCI Bryan Raleigh was destined to recall his comments on the Tower raid with wry amusement.

CHAPTER 9

PRETORIA
Five years later — Friday 25 December, 1998

Christmas day in the Transvaal dawned hot and sunny with clear blue skies. When Mike Reece, wife Christine and daughter Melanie returned with their friends from the mid morning church service in Pretoria's eastern residential suburb, the temperature was already climbing into the high twenties. Like many of their neighbours, they had planned to have a barbecue lunch around the pool, and then have the more traditional British Christmas dinner in the cool of the evening. Mike Reece was General Manager of the Pretoria Diamond Mine, and on their way back from church they had called in for drinks at the home of his underground manager.

Mike was forty-nine, English, and had come to South Africa as a young graduate mining engineer in 1969 to work for the Pretoria Mining Company. Nine years later he had married Christine, a tall athletic ash blonde with cornflower blue eyes. Christine had previously been married to a geologist, but he had been killed in an incident at the Pretoria mine. Mike and Christine had one offspring, a twenty-year-old blond daughter Melanie, who was studying computer science at Wits University in Johannesburg.

Their English friends Paul and Stephanie Remington, with their sixteen-year-old son Jason, were staying with them over the Christmas holiday. The last time they had all met up in South Africa was nearly five years ago. On that occasion, the eleven-year-old Jason and fifteen-year-old Melanie had not got on at all well, the difference of four years between them seeming an unbridgeable gulf. On this second visit, however, Jason, now a tall good-looking lad, was suddenly aware that the intervening years had magically transformed a previously bossy and disdainful girl into something quite breathtaking. After his initial shock, he had become Melanie's willing slave, a situation which secretly flattered the older girl even if she still regarded him as a young boy.

Mike and Christine's ranch-style home was one of ten architect-designed houses in a tree-lined road reminiscent of many similar developments in the Home Counties around London. The house was set back from the road and well screened with yew hedges and evergreen trees. Rose bushes were planted on either side of the curving entrance drive, and in the centre of a circular lawn stood a group of slender jacaranda trees.

Mike drove his Volvo estate up the drive and parked it in front of the double garage. Even though the Volvo was roomy, four of them were squeezed into the back seat, with Melanie sitting on Jason's lap, a situation which the young man found both pleasurable and stimulating.

'Right folks,' announced Mike, 'here's the schedule for lunch. While the male working party gets on with the business of stoking up the braai — that's a barbecue for those of you who don't speak the lingo — the girls get the easy task of taking the meat out of the freezer.'

When they had all clambered out of the car, Christine pointed out the jacaranda trees to Stephanie. 'It's a pity you've never been here in October — those trees are a delight in the Spring with their violet blossoms.'

Stephanie linked arms with Christine as they strolled across to the house. 'Never mind, now it's high summer we can enjoy the scarlet foliage of your poinsettias in the back garden. We only get them at Christmastime in the UK, and they're quite small plants. It's a bit of a shock to see them in South Africa as ten-foot high bushes.'

Mike and Paul had moved round the house to the paved patio at the rear and were busy piling lumps of charcoal on the paper and wood chips they had placed under the grill of a portable barbecue stand. Beyond the patio there was a kidney-shaped pool set in a lawn surrounded by herbaceous borders and backed by fragrant frangipani and purple bougainvillaea.

Mike looked up at the sound of a splash from the pool. Jason and Melanie had already changed into their bathing costumes and were busy playing tag in the water. 'Hey, you two,' he called out, 'you're supposed to be helping with the lunch.'

Paul grinned. 'Let them enjoy themselves — it's the first time Jason's given a member of the opposite sex a second glance, and looking at that handkerchief of a costume Melanie's wearing I can hardly blame him. It's good to see them getting on well together.'

At that moment Stephanie arrived carrying a large dish of steaks and sausages. 'Now then Paul, there'll be time enough for matchmaking when they've both got through university.'

'You're right of course,' agreed Paul. 'These days the chances of them getting through several years of higher education without serious romantic attachments are pretty thin.'

Mike picked up the remaining sheets of a newspaper he had torn up to light the barbecue and began fanning away the smoke that was billowing up from the burning wood. 'I sometimes wonder if getting a barbecue going is worth the effort,' he spluttered.

'Is that you, Mike, making those smoke signals,' complained Christine as she unloaded three bottles of wine and a pile of plates onto the patio table.

'Now don't you start.' Mike turned to Paul. 'When I first came out here I made the mistake of saying I enjoyed a barbecue — after that I was invited to one every few days. By the end of the first month I had several burnt fingers and two singed eyebrows.'

'Please don't exaggerate.' Christine eyed the burning wood critically. 'Men are traditionally supposed to be the fire-makers, but with you I'm not so sure. I think we'd better make a start on the wine while we're waiting.'

At the sound of corks being withdrawn from bottles, Melanie and Jason climbed out of the pool and joined their parents. Jason was some three inches taller than Melanie, his slim boyish frame and white skin contrasting with her well-developed suntanned body. Despite the heat of the afternoon sun he shivered as he towelled himself down.

Melanie poured out two glasses of wine and handed one to Jason. She laid a hand on his chest and felt the muscles beneath his skin tremble under her touch. 'Don't take too much sun for the first few days,' she advised, admiring his youthful frame with approval. 'You've certainly grown since last we met — I can hardly recognise the brat I used to taunt five years ago.'

Jason turned slightly pink and hastily drank some of his wine. 'Well, I do work out in the gym a couple of times a week — and I'm in the school rowing eight,' he ended lamely.

The smoke from the fire slowly cleared, and the steaks and sausages began to sizzle on the wire grill above the barbecue's glowing coals.

'Come on you two,' called Mike. 'The braaivleis is just about ready to eat — so everyone grab a plate and help yourself. There's some salad and mealie-pap on the table.'

Later that afternoon Stephanie joined Christine in the kitchen to help her prepare the evening meal while Mike and Paul had a swim. Melanie had taken Jason in hand and was rubbing sun lotion on his back while he lay flat on his towel. 'Now don't doze off — you've got to do me when I've finished with you,' she admonished.

'My headmaster once said I had an enquiring mind, so I'm open to any suggestions,' Jason replied, surprised at his own boldness.

In the kitchen, Christine loaded the turkey into the oven. She set the timer for eight o'clock and turned to look out of the window. 'Seeing those two young things enjoying themselves made me think of that scary time in London back in 1981.'

'Will I ever forget it!' exclaimed Stephanie. 'When Melanie and I were abducted by those two Russian thugs I really thought our number was up, and it must have been a terrible time for you too, not knowing where Melanie was.'

Christine shuddered at the memory. 'I don't think I slept at all during those three days. Thank God Paul worked out where you were being held, and with Mike and Steven got you both out safely.'

'And all because of a Russian plot to take over the Diamond Syndicate's clients. Have you still got that Daily Telegraph newspaper cutting?'

'Yes, Melanie put it in her scrapbook. At the time she was not quite three and thought the kidnapping was just a game. Because of the Chinese involvement, she labelled the Press cutting 'The Peking Diamonds' affair. Do you remember how excited Mike's aunt Muriel was to be involved in that business? '

Stephanie smiled and shook her head. 'We were really very sad when we heard she'd died just after our last visit here — we'd all become very attached to her. Mike told me she left him her London flat.'

'Yes, that was very sweet of her to include him in her will. We've decided not to sell the flat. When Mike eventually retires we're planning to move back to the UK. As you know, Muriel's apartment overlooks the Thames. It'll make a perfect base for us right in the heart of London.'

Mike stuck his head through the open kitchen door and pointed to his watch. 'It's nearly five o'clock, girls — that's three o'clock UK time. TV1 are relaying the Sky News transmission of the Queen's Christmas message, and there's a rumour she's going to make a special statement. I'll turn the set in the lounge round so we can watch it through the french windows.'

Paul helped Christine and Stephanie arrange the chairs in a semi-circle on the patio, while Mike switched on the TV set and selected the Transvaal TV1 channel. Jason sat down next to Melanie.

'Do you still have those boring discussion programmes on TV where they alternate between English and Afrikaans?' he asked.

'No, those ended some time ago. After the elections, Afrikaans finally lost out to English as the main language of government. I certainly resented having to learn it at school as a second language.'

Christine shook her finger at Melanie. 'That's a very biased view — several of our best friends are Afrikaaners, and they had to become proficient in English as their second language.'

Jason turned back to Melanie. 'What about the rest of your TV programmes — are they any better now?'

'Well, we have more films and UK programmes. Until recently we got your Sky News every morning. Then it was replaced by CNN News, and now we have to endure the tortured vowels of the American presenters.'

'That's a bit acerbic, Melanie.'

'Acerbic, my eye — and that's just a minor irritation. You should try living here for a bit. As a tourist you only see the best side of the country.'

Melanie tossed her head, her blond curls tumbling around the soft curve of her neck. Jason smiled. He liked the way Melanie's cornflower blue eyes flashed when she was angry. 'OK, I know there are lots of things that could be improved here, but it's still a great country and you have a good standard of living. You should try visiting the UK in the winter, and for good measure experience a train or a postal strike.'

The Sky News programme had just began, and the screen showed a view of the royal standard fluttering from the battlements of Balmoral Castle in the Scottish highlands, accompanied by the playing of the national anthem. Then the picture dissolved to one of the Queen sitting in an armchair in her study. On one side they could see the flames of a log fire burning in the grate, and beyond that there was a view of a snow-covered lawn through one of the windows. The television camera slowly zoomed in to a head and shoulders view of the Queen as she turned to smile at her world-wide audience.

'May I first of all wish you a very happy Christmas wherever you may be. This year I am going to depart from the traditional pattern of my previous Christmas messages to you. Instead of reviewing events of the past year, I am going to look ahead to events which will be happening at the end of this century and at the beginning of the next millennium.'

The Queen paused briefly while the camera zoomed closer. 'After much personal contemplation and following long consultations with my family and my advisers, I have decided to lay down the burdens of the monarchy at the end of next year, and to abdicate the throne in favour of a younger member of my family. In making this decision, I have been influenced by the fact that my reign, despite an occasional annus horribilis, has been a particularly long and happy one. I have also felt that the time has come when I should attempt to take over the functions my mother fulfilled so admirably in the past as Queen Mother. However, what I am about to say to you now may surprise many people.'

The Queen paused again, as if hesitant to finally put into words what was on her mind. 'For several years now, my son, Prince Charles, has indicated his reluctance to succeed me as sovereign and ruler of the United Kingdom. Although he has been brought up and educated for this great task, I can well understand that his own personal life and interests have become of great importance to him, and that these would have to be sacrificed should he decide to succeed me and become king.'

'In keeping with his wishes, and in consultation with my husband Prince Philip, the Privy Counsel, the Archbishop of Canterbury, and the Prime Minister, I have decided to abdicate at midnight on the thirty-first of December next year in favour of my grandson Prince William. Until my grandson attains his majority a few months later, I also intend to appoint his uncle, Prince Andrew, as Regent. In nominating Prince William to be your next king, I have looked at past precedents in which the line of succession has been amended for various reasons.'

The Queen opened a book which was lying on her lap. 'In our own royal family tree, for example, William III and his wife Mary II had no children. An act of parliament was already in force which prevented a catholic, or anyone married to a catholic, from being sovereign of England. Because of this situation, an Act of Succession had to be introduced in 1701 which transferred the succession to the protestant descendants of the Hanover line.'

Queen Elizabeth closed the book and turned to the camera again. 'Guided by this precedent, and that of the abdication of my uncle, Edward VIII, the next session of parliament will pass an Act of Succession which will vest the line of inheritance in Prince William. This will be followed at the end of next year by the Declaration of Abdication Act in which I will formally renounce the throne. It is also my wish for the coronation of Prince William to take place in the early Spring of the year 2,000. The next twelve months will provide a very necessary period of orientation for both my grandson, Prince William and his uncle, Prince Andrew, in order that they can face their future duties with confidence. I am sure they can rely on your good wishes as they prepare for their new roles. It only remains for me now to wish you once again a very happy Christmas and a rewarding New Year.'

The picture of the Queen dissolved to an aerial view of Balmoral Castle and the snowy landscape of the Cairngorm mountains.

Mike got up and switched off the television set. 'That was a bit of a surprise, particularly as up to now there's been no leak about a possible change in succession — just rumours.'

Stephanie nodded. 'Perhaps a new start with Prince William will bring back an era of more stable relationships in the royal family. He seems to be a very level-headed young man.'

Melanie chimed in. 'I think he's gorgeous — but what will he be called? The Queen mentioned there was a William III. Will that make him King William IV?'

Paul shook his head. 'No, there's already been a William IV — he reigned around 1830. Prince William will become King William V.'

Christine looked puzzled. 'I wonder why the Queen is spending Christmas at Balmoral this year — she usually broadcasts her message from Sandringham.'

Paul nodded. 'You're right. Perhaps it's because Prince Charles has taken up permanent residence there — they say he's become a bit of a green-welly recluse.'

'Well, with Diana settled in New York and enjoying the adulation of that city's high society, it seems they've both found their ideal life styles,' commented Stephanie. 'I wonder if they'll both be present at the crowning of Prince William.'

'Wouldn't it be great if we could all be in Westminster Abbey for the coronation,' exclaimed Christine.

Jason laughed. 'We'd either have to be peers of the realm, ex-prime ministers, members of parliament, foreign rulers, or at the very least distinguished members of the public. With respect, I don't think any of us qualifies at the moment.'

CHAPTER 10

BRAZIL
Seven months later — Tuesday 3 August, 1999

Leo Vandam climbed crabwise down the steep companion-way of the Varig Boeing 777, his arthritic hip joints paining him after the inaction of the long flight from Cape Town. When he reached the concrete apron of Rio de Janeiro's International airport he pulled down the brim of his fedora against the glare of the early morning sun and slipped on his sunglasses. Leo was in a bad mood. He was hot and uncomfortable in the dark grey suit he had felt compelled to wear for his unscheduled visit to Brazil, and the overnight flight had been far from restful with severe turbulence throwing the big plane around as if it were weightless.

Two days ago Leo had received a phone call from Roman Perez's son Juan. The young man informed him that his father had just died from a massive heart attack, and invited him to attend the funeral. When Leo tried to excuse himself on the grounds of pressing business in Cape Town, Juan's tone had turned icy.

'It is most important to me that you attend,' he said. 'There are things you and I must discuss concerning your business arrangements with my father. If you refuse to meet me, I may be forced to reveal certain facts to the police — facts which I am sure you would prefer to remain confidential. The funeral is on Wednesday — I will send a car to meet you at the airport.' Before Leo could reply, Juan Perez had disconnected.

Leo had only brought hand luggage with him for the overnight stay in Brazil and was quickly through immigration and customs. When he emerged from the customs hall a uniformed chauffeur elbowed his way through the crowd of people meeting arrivals and held up a card with his name on. The man took his case and escorted him to a black Mercedes limousine in the parking area.

'We go straight to the church at Teresopolis for Senor Perez's funeral,' he said.

Leo grunted in reply. Relaxing in the car's air-conditioned luxury, he settled himself back against the yielding upholstery and gazed moodily out of the tinted windows. During the ninety-minute drive, the car wound its way along the serpentine coast road to the north-west of Rio de Janeiro, climbing slowly up the escarpment from sea level to a narrow pass cut through the mountain range. The route was a familiar one to Leo who had made several such journeys over the last few years when visiting his wealthy client.

Despite the spectacular views of the sea visible through the trees at each turn of the road, Leo's eyelids began to droop, and he was soon fast asleep, his chin resting on his chest. Half an hour later, a sudden change in the car's engine note woke him up as they emerged from the tree line and began driving between the steep rocky sides of the pass.

Twenty minutes later they reached Teresopolis and drove through the town's bustling high street. Two miles further on, the chauffeur made a left turn and drove up a steep tree-lined road. As they rounded a bend at the top of the small hill, the pink sandstone church of Santa Bento came into view perched high on a rocky plateau. The church, though small, was ornately decorated with balastraded balconies and baroque carvings. Its roof and its twin towers were clad in multi-coloured tiles which glinted in the sun.

When they drove into the small car park adjoining the church, Leo was surprised to see the number of cars that had already arrived. The chauffeur got out and opened the rear door for Leo who climbed out and flexed his stiff limbs. Leo had spent half his life in the army, and the rest of it in the KGB. Under Stalin's iron rule neither of these organisations had encouraged an interest in religion. Feeling strangely out of place, he walked towards the church and joined the tail end of the group of well-dressed men and women who were being greeted by Juan Perez at the entrance.

Juan Perez, a tall bronzed man in his early thirties with jet black curly hair and deep-set brown eyes made a handsome figure under the ornately carved archway of the church. As befitted the occasion he was dressed in a dark grey suit with a silver cravat at his throat. Juan's lips parted in a thin smile as Leo approached him.

'I am pleased you decided to come,' he said, taking Leo's hand in a limp handshake. He turned and gestured in the direction of the congregation sitting in the body of the church. 'As you can see, my father was a pillar of Rio society.'

Leo was beginning to feel the heat after the air-conditioned comfort of the car. He took out his handkerchief and mopped his bald pate. 'Your father was clearly well thought of — I will miss him as a friend.'

Juan dropped his voice. 'Let us be honest with each other. Both of us will miss his money — but we'll talk of that problem later. First we must suffer the formalities of the burial service and the eulogies.'

Leo was relieved to find a seat at the rear of the church. The vaulted stone arches loomed cool and lofty above him and he could smell the sweet heavy scent rising from the carved wooden censer hanging in the sacristy. The Roman Catholic priest began intoning the burial service in Latin, a language Leo only dimly remembered from his school days, and he had difficulty in staying awake. Then one of Roman Perez's business colleagues spoke of his commercial and civic careers in Portuguese, which was not among Leo's limited range of modern languages. The two hymns that were sung during the service sounded vaguely familiar to him, and he found himself moving his lips silently in response to the music.

After the service, the priest, followed by four bearers carrying the coffin, and Juan Perez as chief mourner, led the congregation out of the church to the sloping site of the small graveyard. Using silk ropes, the bearers lowered the brass embellished ebony coffin slowly to its resting place in the stony ground while a tenor sang Ave Maria.

One by one, the friends and business acquaintances of Roman Perez filed past his final resting place, some of the now weeping women dropping a flower into the grave. When everyone but Leo had departed, Juan went down on one knee at the grave side. He took a handful of soil and tossed it onto the coffin.

'Goodbye, my father,' he murmured, half to himself. 'Now at last I can begin to live.' Then he turned to Leo. 'We'll go back to the house together and have some lunch. After that I have something to show you.'

Leo pointed to the departing members of the congregation. 'What about your father's relatives and associates, aren't you inviting them back to the house?'

'My father has no surviving relative but me.' Juan gave a bitter laugh. 'He was an only child, which makes me the last of the Perez line — and good riddance some people will say. As for his friends and associates, they've drunk the last of his wine as far as I'm concerned.'

Juan dismissed the chauffeur and climbed into a yellow beach buggy. He started the engine and waited impatiently for Leo to struggle into the bucket seat beside him. Then he raced out of the car park in a shower of gravel, and swung into the road which led down from the church. At the bottom of the hill, several cars were still waiting to get out into the main road. Juan came to a halt and sounded his horn angrily. Then with Leo hanging on grimly to the sides of his seat he swung out and bucketed down alongside the queue of cars. At the bottom, he shot out into the main road and skidded through a gap in the oncoming line of traffic.

The Perez home was four miles from the centre of Teresopolis in a small valley which formed an exclusive 'Shangri La' for a group of millionaire-owned properties built within the shelter of a high-security perimeter wall. Each of the buildings on this secluded estate had been built in a different style. The Perez two-storey homestead had been designed by a Spanish architect, and had two enormous living areas. The ground floor room opened out onto a paved terrace which was built around an oval swimming pool, its floor paved with light and dark blue tiles arranged in a starfish pattern. The upper room was also designed for open-air living and had a large balcony running the length of the house. Beyond the swimming pool, manicured lawns swept down to an ornamental pool surrounded by tropical plants and flowering bushes.

Juan drove his beach buggy through the archway entrance into the grounds of the house and followed the driveway past the swimming pool. As they rounded the house Leo could see a group of humming birds hovering around the blossoms of the tropical plants, their long delicate beaks extracting nectar from deep inside the flowers. When Juan came to the four-car garage built onto the side of the house he slowed and pressed a button on a remote control unit. One of the doors opened obediently and he drove inside and parked between a red Ferrari sports car and a white Porsche.

'I'll probably have to sell both of these beauties.' Juan got out of the buggy and stroked the bonnets of the two cars while Leo levered himself out of his seat. 'Father was less than generous to me in his will — but let's have lunch first. We can talk finance later.'

He led Leo through a door at the rear of the garage and up a flight of stairs into the upper living area. A picnic lunch had been set out for them on one of the tables on the balcony above the terrace. Leo grunted approvingly at the sight of dishes containing cold meats, chicken breasts, king prawns and a variety of salads and fruits.

'I see your cook and housekeeper are looking after you well,' he commented.

Juan picked up a plate and began helping himself to the food. 'I can't complain. My father lived simply, and rarely entertained, but he did keep a passable cellar. Can I pour you a glass of his favourite Mouton Cadet, or would you prefer a white wine?'

'The Rothschilds cabernet will do fine,' agreed Leo, and forked a generous selection of chicken and cold meats onto his plate. When they had eaten, Juan rang a handbell, and the housekeeper brought them two cups, a glass caffetaire of coffee and a jug of cream.

Leo sipped his coffee appreciatively. 'I would have killed for such coffee in that terrible winter when we were trying to break through the German lines around Leningrad.'

Juan lit up a cigarette, and blew a smoke ring out over the balcony. 'On one of the few occasions we spoke together, my father talked of your wartime exploits — it seems he thought highly of you.'

Leo's face wrinkled in a rare smile. 'I'm pleased to hear of his opinion. Although Senor Perez and I were mainly business associates, he also spoke of you Juan. I have no family, but it saddened me to hear of your disagreements.'

Juan sighed. 'I never knew my mother, and when I was young my father was always busy. I had everything but his time, and the friends I made as I grew up were not to his liking. All of which brings me to the business in hand. Because of my father's strong disapproval of my lifestyle, he has left all of his money and his property in trust for me — I get the same monthly allowance which I found totally inadequate even when he was alive.'

Leo shrugged his broad shoulders, and helped himself to more coffee. 'I'm sorry to hear that — there must surely be more assets than just the cars which you can sell off. What about the collection of paintings I have seen around the house on previous visits?'

'Everything in this house is part of the estate and included in the trust fund. I'm not allowed to touch a single thing.'

Juan moved closer to Leo and dropped his voice. 'Now I can tell you the real reason I wanted you here. Three days ago, when I was checking through my father's desk, I found an envelope containing a key and one of my father's business cards. The key didn't fit any of the locks in the house, and the card had a six-digit number written on the back. When I showed the key to the housekeeper, she said she thought it might belong to the door of a small room in the basement. My father apparently used to spend an hour or two in the room each week, but he always locked himself in. He told the housekeeper it was a photographic dark room.'

Leo smiled grimly. 'I will make a guess that what you discovered in the room had nothing to do with photography.'

Juan nodded. 'Inside the room I found the walls were covered with paintings. One of them I remember being reported as stolen a few years ago. As none of the pictures had ever been displayed in the house, I guessed that they were probably all the result of burglaries. However, that was not all. Hidden behind one of the pictures was a small wall safe. I tried using the six-digit number on the safe's combination lock, but with no result. Then I remembered my father was an enthusiast for puzzles and codes. When I was a young child he once encoded my birth date and asked me to work backwards and discover the code he had used. I was only seven at the time, and to his disgust it took me several hours to crack his code. Eventually I came up with the answer. He had added one to each digit in my birth date and subtracted the result from ten.'

Juan paused and poured himself more coffee. 'I used the code on the six-digit number that was on the back of the business card, and dialled the resulting number into the combination lock. This time the safe door opened. Inside it I found two large diamonds and a bundle of papers.'

Leo sighed. 'The yellow diamond you found in the safe is the Golconda d'Or which was stolen from a Sydney exhibition in 1983. The big colourless diamond has not as yet been reported as missing.'

'I assume that the paintings and the diamonds are all items you obtained for my father's clandestine collection?'

'I will only say that I knew of their existence,' admitted Leo.

'That's nonsense, and you know it,' sneered Juan, his voice hardening. 'The bundle of papers in the safe is a complete record of the correspondence and accounts between you and my father. It links you firmly to the theft of the two diamonds and to several of the paintings.'

Leo's face darkened in anger. He picked up an apple from a dish of fruit on the table. 'So what do you intend to do about it?'

'Nothing, providing you co-operate. I'm desperately short of funds. The diamonds are the most portable and valuable part of my father's hidden assets. I suggest you take them and sell them for me.'

Leo tossed the apple in the air and caught it again. 'That's absurd — both diamonds are far too well known. Nobody will touch them.' He paused in thought. 'In the case of the Golconda d'Or, however, the police have assumed the diamond has already been cut into smaller gems and disposed of.'

'Then that's just what I want you to arrange for me. Get both of the diamonds re-cut, and then find buyers for me — and do it quickly.'

Leo's grip tightened on the apple until his knuckles showed white. 'I can get the yellow diamond re-cut, but slicing up the big one would be an act of vandalism. You would be destroying history.'

'History was never my favourite subject. You have two choices my friend — either you do my bidding, or the papers linking you to the thefts will be sent to the Cape Town police via Interpol.'

By now Leo's face had turned scarlet with rage and the veins on his neck were bulging. He staggered to his feet, knocking over his chair. 'If you do that, I will crush you like this apple.'

Juan stared with fascination as the fingers of Leo's right hand tightened their grip on the apple and slowly crushed it to a pulp. Leo dumped the mangled fruit on the table and towered over the young man.

'Please calm down, my friend,' exclaimed Juan, raising both hands to defend himself. 'There is no need for such anger between us. I am willing to split any money from such a venture on a fifty-fifty basis. If the recut stones are marketed carefully, that could amount to many millions of US dollars for us both.'

Leo snorted and reluctantly sat down again. He grabbed a table napkin and wiped his hand. 'You are right of course. Sentiment must bow to commerce. As you suggest, I will take the diamonds and find a suitable cutter. But you in turn must be patient. I will get the yellow stone cut first, but the big one will have to be handled with great discretion. If your father had lived, I know he had other plans for the big stone.'

Juan shook his head. 'I have suffered his plans for too long.' He held out his hand. 'So we have a deal then.'

Leo took the young man's hand. 'Yes we have a deal. Now take me down to your father's vault and show me the two diamonds — many years have passed since I delivered them into his hands.'

CHAPTER 11

CAPE TOWN — ANTWERP
Wednesday 4 August, 1999

When Leo Vandam returned to Cape Town after his stormy meeting with Juan Perez in Teresopolis, he knew he had a problem on his hands. Clive Drake collected him from the airport that evening and realised from Leo's taciturn manner that it was not the right time to question him on his visit. On arrival at the Eagles Nest, Clive parked the car in the garage. He got Leo's hand luggage out of the boot and followed his boss into the lift cabin. When they reached the terrace level, Leo got out of the cabin and grabbed his case from Clive. He stormed into the house and bellowed for Oleg Antonovitch.

When the three of them were assembled in the lounge, Leo unzipped his case and removed a small cardboard box. He took the lid off the box and lifted out a grey cloth bundle. Leo walked across to a glass-topped coffee table in front of the lounge's large picture window. The sun was just setting on the horizon, and threw a golden glow across the room, tinting the white leather lounge suite pink, and bringing the canvases on the wall alive with vibrant colours.

Leo placed the cloth bundle on the coffee table and beckoned his associates closer. He carefully unfolded the cloth and revealed a ninety-four carat emerald-cut yellow diamond and a five-hundred and thirty carat pear-shaped white diamond.

Oleg was the first to break the silence. He picked up the yellow stone. 'I last saw this in the Sydney exhibition. It's the Golconda d'Or.'

Clive reached forward and picked up the large colourless stone. He held it up to catch the last rays of the sun before its golden rim was extinguished by the sea. 'The Cullinan I,' he murmured reverently.

'Ten out of ten for recognition,' snarled Leo sarcastically. 'That young Perez pup wants me to have both of these sliced up and recut. Then he wants me to find a buyer — the idiot is short of money as usual, and in his father's will the entire family fortune has been left in trust, so he can't touch the capital.'

Clive laid the Cullinan I carefully back on the table. 'But you can't destroy the Star of Africa — that would be unforgivable. I thought Roman Perez was going to return it eventually.'

Leo laughed bitterly. 'Yes, I know — but the grim reaper got to him first. Now his son is threatening to expose us all to the police unless we do what he wants. These two diamonds were not the only objects in Roman Perez's safe. There was also a complete dossier on all our transactions with him.'

Oleg replaced the Golconda d'Or on the table. 'So, what you decide to do, boss?'

Leo carefully wrapped both diamonds back in the cloth and put them in his case. 'I haven't much choice. I told Juan it would be very difficult to find a cutter prepared to touch the Cullinan. The Golconda d'Or is another matter. After all this time, the assumption is it's already been recut and disposed of. Juan has agreed to this stone being recut first, and a buyer found for the resulting gems. That gives the Cullinan a reprieve for the time being.'

Clive's eyes glinted behind his thick-lensed glasses. 'Perhaps the young Perez heart will soften, or even fail, before we need to consider the big stone.'

Leo grunted. 'There is always that possibility — but we must make sure we get the incriminating documents from him first. In the meanwhile, I want you, Oleg, to accompany me to Antwerp tomorrow. There we will take the yellow diamond to an old diamantaire acquaintance of mine by the name of Max Goldberg. I helped him leave Russia just before the breakup of the USSR. He can be a tricky customer, so I want you to guard my back.'

* * *

Max Goldberg was one of the small band of Jewish diamantaires who were allowed to leave Russia in the late '70s. They re-established their diamond businesses in Israel and Belgium, and for a time were able to use their connection with the Soviet Foreign Trade Association, Russalmaz, to purchase uncut Russian diamonds at an attractive discount.

Max's diamond cutting office and workshop was one of several similar operations housed in a building in Antwerp's Pelikaan Straat, and situated conveniently close to the main railway station. The task of producing a polished faceted diamond from the rough stone is usually shared by up to six specialists. The designer, who is often the owner of the business, inspects the uncut gem and decides how it can be most profitably sawn or cleaved. The cleaver and the sawyer then divide the diamond up following his instructions, and pass the results to the bruter who fashions the rounded or fancy-cut profile of the gem. The final faceting work is performed by the cross-worker and the brillianteerer who between them grind and polish the various crown and pavilion facets on the stone.

Max Goldberg's workforce was small, however, consisting of himself as designer, a sawyer who also acted as a cleaver, a bruter who doubled as cross-worker and brillianteerer, and a typist.

When Leo and Oleg arrived in Max's office on Friday morning, the only person in the outer office was his typist. 'Mr Goldberg will be with you in a few minutes,' she said. 'He's busy at the moment checking a problem stone with our sawyer. Please take a seat.'

Oleg had never been in a diamond polisher's premises before, and looked about him with interest at the contents of the small office. Against one wall an old oak bookcase contained a small library of volumes on diamond cutting and grading. On top of the bookcase there were glass models showing the various stages in the cutting and faceting of a round brilliant-cut diamond. Alongside these were full size replicas in glass of the 3,106 carat Cullinan rough, and the nine principal stones cut from it.

Leo walked across and picked up one of the models showing the development of the brilliant cut's fifty seven facets. 'I learned quite a bit about this business from Max when he was running his diamond works in Moscow. How to grade a polished diamond in the four Cs of colour, clarity, cut and carat weight. The intimate knowledge of the market that is essential when pricing a diamond.' He replaced the glass model and chuckled. 'He even told me how some diamond polishers increment their wages by a practice known in the trade as growing a diamond.'

Oleg looked up in surprise. 'How can diamonds grow?'

'It's quite simple. The polisher acquires a very small uncut diamond chip, perhaps as small as five points — that's five-hundredths of a carat. In his leisure moments, when the boss is not looking, he polishes it into a tiny brilliant cut gem, carefully weighs it, and puts it away. Then he waits until his boss gives him a slightly larger chip to polish which is the same colour and quality as his own small stone. If the diamond he polishes from this chip weighs a fraction of a carat more than his own small stone, he substitutes one for the other. In this way, and with patience, his own small diamond can be made to grow after many such substitutions, from five points to perhaps twenty-five points — that's a quarter of a carat!'

'And his boss does not find out?' asked Oleg.

'Not unless he has time to watch his staff every minute of the day.'

At this moment Max came into the office. 'Leo, you old rogue — it's good to see you again.'

Apart from Max's close-cropped greying hair and beard, he and Leo could have been brothers. They were both in their sixties, with contours betraying signs of the over-indulgence which often comes with success. The two men embraced each other.

'How long has it been?' asked Leo.

'Don't ask — let's let's just say we're both a lot older and wiser since we last met in Moscow.'

'You certainly look more prosperous, Max, since you emigrated to the West — how's business in the diamond world today?'

'Not so good, Leo. The market is low at the moment. If I found a diamond in the gutter, polished it and sold it, I would still make a loss.'

Leo laughed, and introduced Max to Oleg. 'This is one of my

men from the old KGB days. He looks after my security arrangements in Cape Town.'

Max nodded, and turned to his typist. 'Please go to lunch now — I will take care of the office.' When the girl had gone, he sat down behind his desk and waved Leo and Oleg to the two chairs in the small reception area.

'My sawyer and his colleagues are busy on rush orders in the workshop, so we won't be interrupted. Now, what is this business you spoke of on the telephone yesterday?'

Leo removed a small white cotton pouch from his pocket. He untied the draw cord and shook out the yellow Golconda d'Or onto the palm of his hand. 'I want you to re-cut this into six round brilliants of equal size.'

Max took the stone from him. A surprised expression of recognition passed across his face. 'I remember this diamond. Many people have speculated over its fate since it disappeared in 1980.' He pulled a hand lens from his pocket and held it close to his right eye while he sighted into the stone, turning it about to check for possible flaws. He put the lens away again, and shook his head sadly. 'It's a beautiful stone, but to do what you ask would diminish its value ten-fold at least.'

Leo shrugged his broad shoulders. 'What else can one do with such a well-known stone? My client needs the money desperately.'

Max sighed. 'Of course I can divide the stone up as you suggest, but such a task would be very expensive, and I have to take into account the risk I will be running in knowingly handling a famous stolen diamond of this size. I will also have to pay my staff extra for their silence.'

'For your expenses and to compensate for the risk, you can keep one of the six diamonds, plus any chips.'

Max considered this for a few minutes and did some sums on his calculator. Then he made up his mind. 'I accept your terms, Leo, but with my present commitments I won't be able to start work on the stone for at least another month. However, I promise that in two months time I will deliver to you in Cape Town five beautifully faceted round brilliants. You have my word on this.'

The two men shook hands on the deal. Leo handed over the

linen pouch, and Max dropped the stone in it and put it in his office safe. 'Now let me take you both out to lunch. There's a quiet little bistro round the corner where we can indulge in a few reminiscences while we eat. Incidentally, I'm off to the UK on the eleventh of this month to be present in Cornwall for the total eclipse of the sun — why don't you and Oleg take a few days off and join me.'

'An eclipse of the sun — now that could be a good omen for our joint enterprise. I could do with a holiday, but I'm afraid I cannot risk Oleg's presence in the UK. His photofit picture is still on police files after his participation in the Sydney exhibition robbery.'

Max laughed. 'With the Golconda d'Or sitting in my safe, it would certainly be a cruel stroke of fate if some diligent UK policeman saw him in my company!'

'That would not be good for my digestion,' agreed Leo. He smiled as a thought struck him. 'While I'm in the UK I could also take the opportunity of visiting the scene of my greatest triumph — the Tower of London!'

Oleg turned to Max. 'Before we leave, I would much like to see your workshop.'

'That would be only a pleasure, my friend,' said Max.

He led the two men through a door into a room behind the small office. The workshop was much larger than the office, and in its centre there was a row of six sawing machines, attended by a thin angular man dressed in a brown protective coat.

Max introduced them to the man. 'This is my sawyer. His main work is to saw the stones in half following the guide lines I draw on them in indian ink. Those small phosphor-bronze saw blades you see on each machine are turning at around three-thousand rpm. He keeps their cutting edges coated with a mixture of oil and diamond dust. When he's not watching the machines, he will sometimes act as a cleaver. Cleaving is mainly used on larger stones, and then only if the cleaving direction results in a good yield.'

'What is difference?' asked Oleg.

'Sawing can take a long time — maybe a whole day to divide a one-carat stone in two. Cleaving is instantaneous. A groove called a kerf is cut along the surface of the stone in the right place, and the cleaving blade is inserted in it and given a sharp tap. If everything is correct, the stone parts in two. If not, it breaks into little pieces, and I fire the cleaver,' replied Max with a grin.

Then he showed Oleg the small lathe-type machine where his bruter was busy rounding off the corners on a sawn stone to produce a circular profile prior to faceting. 'You notice he is using a small chip of diamond mounted on the end of that wooden dop as a cutting tool.'

Oleg looked over the bruter's shoulder. 'Just like machine tool on lathe,' he commented.

Max nodded and pointed across to the far corner of the workshop where there was a sturdy bench holding four motor-driven cast-iron polishing scaifes. 'Those are high-speed grinding and polishing laps. This is where my bruter uses his other cutting skills as a cross-worker and brillianteerer.'

'These cast-iron plates are also coated with diamond powder?' asked Oleg.

'Yes — he first uses a coarse grade to grind the crown and pavilion facets on the stones he has rounded off on the bruting lathe, and then a finer grade to put the final high polish on each facet,' answered Max.

'If you buy one carat rough diamond and polish it, what size is finished diamond?'

Max shrugged his shoulders. 'I would be lucky to get half a carat of polished stones from a one carat rough diamond. Half the weight is lost in cutting, so after several days' work I might have a faceted diamond weighing one-third of a carat, plus a small one less than half that weight.'

'But you still make good profit?' asked Oleg.

'I would if I were also a retail jeweller, but I sell my output of polished stones to a diamond dealer, who then supplies a manufacturing jeweller. By the time my one carat rough is polished and eventually sold in a jeweller's shop in Hatton Garden it will have increased in value by up to eight times.'

Oleg was suitably impressed, but by now Leo was beginning to feel hungry. Before Oleg could ask any more questions, he waved a protesting finger at Max. 'I know what you are up to, you sly old devil. Soon you will persuade my colleague he has missed his vocation in life, and then I will lose a valuable member of my staff.'

He put his arm round Oleg and guided him firmly towards the door. 'I think this is a good time for us to visit that quiet little bistro you mentioned earlier, Max.'

CHAPTER 12

LONDON
Thursday 9 September, 1999

The Chairman of the Diamond Syndicate, Sir James Crichton, sat uneasily in the anti-room of the Prime Minister's study in 10 Downing Street. Sir James was in his early seventies, and in his dark grey pin-stripe suit, white silk shirt and black tie embellished with a pattern of tiny white diamonds he could easily have been mistaken for one of the PM's senior civil servants. His silver-grey hair was neatly groomed, but his gold-rimmed spectacles had slipped forward undetected onto the bridge of his nose, a sure indication of his state of perplexity. A copy of the Times lay unopened on the table in front of him, and although he gazed at its restrained headlines he found he was unable to concentrate on any of the news items.

When he arrived in his office that morning just before nine o'clock he had been surprised to receive a phone call from the Prime Minister's private secretary requesting him to attend a meeting in 10 Downing street at ten am. The short notice of the summons and the tone of the secretary's request had implied it was more of a command than an invitation.

The last time Sir James had a meeting with a senior government minister was in 1981. On that memorable occasion it was with the foreign secretary, and Sir James was the one who had initiated the meeting to produce evidence of Russia's involvement in a plot to discredit the Syndicate and take over its clients. Today he was given no reason why he had been summoned to Downing Street. Perhaps, he mused, it had something to do with the diamond trade figures, but in that case the meeting would have been called by the chancellor of the exchequer. At that moment his reverie was interrupted by the opening of the study door.

'The Prime Minister is ready to see you now,' said the private secretary.

As Sir James was ushered into the study, a tall fair-haired man in his late fifties got up from behind his desk and walked forward to greet him with outstretched hand.

'Good morning, Sir James. Thank you for responding so promptly to my call.' The Prime Minister waved his hand at another man sitting on the far side of the desk. 'I think you know Roger Nathan, the Home Secretary.'

When the two men had exchanged greetings the Prime Minister pointed to another chair in front of his desk. 'Please make yourself comfortable Sir James. The Commissioner of Police is due any moment. While we're waiting perhaps you would care for some coffee?'

Sir James nodded and the PM pressed a key on his intercom unit. A few seconds later a young woman came in carrying a tray of cups and a thermos jug. The PM waited until the coffee had been served and the study door was closed again. 'The reason I asked you to attend this meeting, Sir James, was to enlist your advice as a diamond expert.'

'Always pleased to be of assistance,' responded the Diamond Syndicate's chairman.

The door opened again, and the private secretary ushered in the Commissioner of Police, Sir Noel Lancaster.

'Good to see you, Noel — please take a seat.' The PM glanced at the three men sitting in front of him. 'Now that we're all present, Roger will explain the serious situation he has just been made aware of.'

The Home Secretary put his finger to his lips and got to his feet. He switched on the light, walked over to the window, and pulled the curtains across. 'Can't be too careful in these hi-tech days,' he explained as he returned to his seat. 'Conversations can be picked up from the vibrations produced in a pane of glass. Now, to get down to business. As the PM has just mentioned, a serious problem has suddenly come to light. You will be aware that a considerable amount of planning is currently taking place in preparation for the coronation of Prince William next March.'

The Home Secretary put his hand in his jacket pocket and pulled out a white leather pouch.

'In preparation for the coronation ceremony, the crown jewellers have been checking and cleaning the royal regalia over the last few days. Yesterday, the jeweller who was handling the royal sceptre noticed that the Cullinan I — that's the large pear-shaped diamond mounted near the top of the sceptre — was slightly loose in its gold wire mount.'

'In case you are unaware of the fact, as I must confess I was, when the royal sceptre was modified back in 1910 to take the Cullinan I, the design allowed for the stone to be unclipped from the sceptre and worn separately. The thin gold wire mount I have just mentioned is almost invisible from the front when the diamond is clipped into the sceptre, but from the rear you can see a small loop at the top from which the stone can be suspended as a pendant. Well, when the jeweller unclipped the diamond from the sceptre he realised that the stone felt unusually heavy. Puzzled by this, he carefully removed the gold wire holder and weighed the stone. It should have registered a weight of exactly 530.2 carats. The stone he placed on his balance weighed just over 888 carats.'

The PM turned to Sir James. 'As I understand it, at that weight the stone could not possibly be a diamond.'

'That's correct.' Sir James extracted a small calculator from his breast pocket, and punched in some numbers. 'Diamond has a specific gravity of 3.52. If what appears to be an imitation of the Cullinan has been cut to the same dimensions as the real stone, and weighs 888 carats...,' he paused and peered at the result of his calculations, 'then the imitation is roughly 1.67 times heavier than the Cullinan I, and has a specific gravity of about 5.9. The only diamond simulant having that value is cubic zirconium oxide, or CZ for short.'

The Home Secretary untied the drawstring on the white leather pouch he had been holding in his hand, and tipped out what appeared to be the Cullinan I diamond. He threw the large pear-shaped stone across to Sir James. 'This is the fake stone the jeweller removed from the sceptre. It's certainly far more convincing than the glass and quartz replicas I've been looking at in the Hatton Garden premises of the crown jewellers.'

The Commissioner took the Cullinan replica from Sir James and turned it over in his hands. 'One possible scenario we must consider first concerns the jeweller who discovered the fake Cullinan I. He was, in fact, the last person to handle the sceptre when it was cleaned on the previous occasion. I don't think I have to spell out what's on my mind.'

The Home Secretary sighed. 'The man in question has been with the crown jewellers for over thirty years. He joined from school as an apprentice. No-one, including the staff of the crown jewellers, is allowed access to any item of the royal regalia without the curator of the Tower and the head warden being present. I have checked that this rule was strictly in force on all occasions when the sceptre was being cleaned, including the recent one.'

'I would also like to make the following point about the practicality of substituting a replica for the Cullinan I. Although I mentioned earlier that the diamond can be unclipped from the sceptre, it is not that easy to substitute a replica unless it is fitted with an identical gold wire holder. We now know that after the Cullinan was unlawfully removed from the sceptre, its gold wire mount was detached and then refitted around the replica. Our jewellery experts tell us that this gold wire support had first been cut to release the diamond, and the wire had then been rejoined around the replica by using soft solder. This operation must have taken at least five minutes, and would have been very visible to anybody in the room when the sceptre was being cleaned. I think that answers any doubt you may have in your mind Noel.'

'Thank you, Roger — I take your point.' The Commissioner handed the CZ replica back to him. 'I think we now need to consider all the remaining possibilities and then draw up a plan of action.'

The PM nodded. 'You were quite in order to voice your suspicions, Noel, and I agree we should now look in other directions.' He opened a folder lying on his desk and held up a newspaper cutting for them all to see. 'I'm beginning to believe the extraordinary event which took place in 1994 is as good a starting place as any.'

The banner headline across the top of the cutting read;

ARMED ATTACK ON TOWER — SAS RESCUE CROWN JEWELS

Roger Nathan replaced the Cullinan replica in its leather pouch. 'I'm sure we all agree that the raid on the Tower is the key to this affair. First, however, we must consider the situation in the light of the impending coronation of Prince William. In my opinion, it would be a disaster if news of the theft of the Cullinan I, which is one of the most important symbols in the royal regalia, become known by the general public. The three people in the crown jewellers who were involved in the discovery of the theft have already signed papers relevant to the Official Secrets Act, and of course the keeper, the head warden and the curator have all been made aware of the need for secrecy.'

'I have made arrangements, Prime Minister, for a quartz replica to be mounted in the sceptre, and the lights in the Jewel House be adjusted so as to conceal the problem from visitors to the Jewel House until the real stone has been recovered. Even then I think the affair should continue to be kept secret so that public confidence in our ability to guard the nation's treasures is not undermined.'

The Home Secretary turned to the Commissioner of Police and Sir James. 'I suggest, Noel, we use Detective Chief Inspector Raleigh, who is in charge of the Art and Antiques Investigation Squad, and the two men, Sir James, from your Special Operations department to form an investigation team with the specific task of tracking down the missing diamond and restoring it to the royal sceptre. With the need for secrecy in mind, I further suggest we use the codename 'The Phantom Diamond' in any communication concerning the investigation.' With that he handed the white leather pouch containing the replica to Sir James, and the Prime Minister thanked all those present for attending and closed the meeting.

* * *

When Sir James returned to 2 Manorhouse Street after his meeting at 10 Downing Street, he summoned Paul Remington and Steven Cumings to his office. 'I've just come from a meeting with the Prime Minister.' He looked keenly at both the men sitting in front of him. 'Also present at the meeting were the Home Secretary and the Commissioner of Police, which should convey to you this was not a social occasion.'

Paul leaned forward in his chair. 'I assume your presence and that of the Commissioner means that something to do with the theft of diamonds was involved.'

'You assume correctly.' Sir James' eyes glinted behind his spectacles. 'What I am about to reveal to you now is highly confidential. If word of it leaks out it would severely embarrass both the Government and the Home Office.' He paused and took the white leather pouch from his pocket and laid it on his desk. 'The Crown Jewellers have begun checking and cleaning the royal regalia ready for the coronation of Prince William in March of next year. While they were working on the royal sceptre, one of them unmounted the Cullinan I diamond and discovered it was a CZ fake.'

Steven gave a long low whistle in disbelief. 'You mean the Cullinan has been nicked?' he exclaimed. 'Wow — that must be the crime of the century.'

Sir James glared at him. 'I would have preferred your reaction to have been couched in more responsible language, but in essence I agree with its sentiment. Now, in order to prevent a repeat of the fuss the media made over the raid on the Tower of London five years ago, I cannot stress too strongly that this information must remain strictly confidential. Because of the need for secrecy the investigation into the theft has been codenamed "The Phantom Diamond".'

He looked at Paul. 'You wish to make a comment?'

'Yes, Sir James. Can we assume that in this matter the staff of the crown jewellers are beyond reproach.'

'Yes, I can give you that assurance.'

'Well then, it becomes crystal clear that the only time the sceptre was out of its display case and vulnerable was during the raid on the Tower. There was a period of some seven minutes before the SAS regained control of the Jewel House. However, I'm surprised that the Cullinan could have been unmounted and a replacement substituted in so short a time.'

Sir James nodded in agreement. 'The same thought occurred to me, but I've been told that this is not so difficult as it might seem. The Cullinan unclips from the sceptre, and all that needs to be done then is to remove a gold wire mount from around the stone and refit it around the replica.'

Steven pulled his right ear lobe, a habit he had when puzzled. 'But the royal regalia was checked immediately after the raid. Why wasn't the substitution discovered then?'

Sir James sighed and untied the draw cord of the leather pouch lying on his desk. He slipped out the CZ replica of the Cullinan and handed it to Steven. 'Now do you see why?'

Steven turned the stone over in his hand and then passed it to Paul. 'It certainly looks cosher to me, but my experience of polished diamonds is rather limited.' Under his breath he added, 'on my salary.'

'I'm aware that CZ is much softer than diamond,' commented Paul. 'But its refractive index is high enough to give a convincing internal reflection, and its dispersion is not too dissimilar to diamond's, so what made the crown jewellers suspicious?'

Sir James shrugged his shoulders. 'I understand the stone felt unusually heavy. CZ has a specific gravity around 1.7 times greater than diamond.'

'Do the crown jewellers have any idea who made the replica?'

'Not as far as I'm aware. I seem to remember that it was the Russians who first developed the production technique for growing CZ crystals and subsequently introduced CZ as a diamond simulant.'

Paul handed the replica back to Sir James. 'Russia again,' he commented. 'That's intriguing.'

Sir James put the replica back in its pouch and gave it to Paul. 'This is the only real evidence we have so far, so take care of it. I agree with you that the substitution was most probably made during the raid on the Tower. However, the armed gang perished when the helicopter exploded, and nothing was found on the nine bodies that were recovered, or among the wreckage of the

Chinook.' He paused in thought for a moment. 'Until the diamond is recovered the Sceptre will go back on show to the public with a quartz replica taking the place of the diamond. I'm assured that with appropriate lighting, the public will not notice any difference. In the meanwhile, the Home Secretary has asked me to let the two of you join forces with the man in charge of the Art and Antiques Investigation Squad, and to jointly investigate this affair with the prime objective of recovering the Cullinan I before the coronation in March.'

Steven counted off the time on his fingers. 'That gives us just five months.'

Sir James nodded. 'I suggest you telephone DCI Raleigh at the Yard and get straight down to work — the scent on the "Phantom Diamond" trail is five years cold!'

CHAPTER 13

LONDON — CAPE TOWN
Friday 10 September, 1999

In the Diamond Syndicate's building in Manorhouse Street, Paul Remington's Special Operations section occupied three offices on the second floor alongside the Security Surveillance and Internal Audit departments. This was a convenient arrangement as the work of Paul's section occasionally included discrepancies in the stocks of diamonds within the building. The rest of the floors in the building were divided between various administration offices and the diamond sorting departments responsible for grading the hundreds of thousands of uncut stones purchased by the Syndicate from the world's diamond-producing countries.

The Syndicate's sorting staff of over four-hundred people were employed to sort, grade and value the diamonds into over four thousand categories of colour, quality, shape and weight, in preparation for the five-weekly 'Sights'. It was during these 'Sights' that the brokers, or 'Sight Holders', were invited to No. 2 Manorhouse Street to inspect the allocation of stones based on their requirements or those of their clients.

Although Paul's department was not directly involved with this five-weekly cycle of sorting and selling, he sometimes called on the expertise of one of the managers in the sorting departments. Today, he had asked Jeffrey Hamilton, a tall angular man nearing retirement age who was the chief quality controller, to attend a meeting in his office. Even as a young man, Jeffrey, a gemmologist and a Fellow of the Gemmological Association of Great Britain, had lost most of his hair. Now at sixty years of age, with a bald pate thrusting through a fringe of sandy-coloured hair, he had the appearance of an elderly monk.

When Jeffrey arrived for the meeting that morning, he found

Paul and Steven in earnest conversation with a tall visitor wearing jeans and a loosely fitting crumpled jacket.

'Thanks for coming, Jeffrey,' said Paul. 'Let me introduce you to DCI Bryan Raleigh, head of the Art and Antiques Investigation Squad of the Metropolitan Police.' He paused while the two men shook hands. 'I've asked you here for some technical advice in your capacity as a gemmologist. But first of all I have to apologise as I'm not allowed to give you the full background details of the investigation we are currently engaged on.'

Jeffrey rubbed his bald dome. 'Sounds intriguing — but fire away. What's the problem?'

Paul picked up the white leather pouch and emptied out the replica of the Cullinan I. 'What can you tell us about this — we'd particularly like to know where it was cut.'

Jeffrey took the diamond replica and hefted it in his hand. He pulled a hand lens from his pocket and inspected the junctions of the crown facets. Then, holding the stone up with the large table facet facing him, he slowly tilted the stone away from him until the facet was almost horizontal.

'This is clearly a very convincing replica of the Cullinan I,' he commented. 'From its weight, it must be one of the man-made diamond simulants. Its refractive index is quite high — it almost passes the tilt test for diamond.'

Jeffrey extracted a pen-shaped reflectivity probe from his breast pocket and applied its sensor tip to the replica's table facet. 'As I thought,' he added. 'It's a CZ.'

Paul took the stone back from Jeffrey. 'That's what we were told — thanks for the confirmation. Now, have you any idea where it could have been cut?'

Jeffrey blew out his cheeks. 'That's a bit more difficult. For a start, this is the first model of the Cullinan I I've seen that's been cut from cubic zirconium oxide — that's the proper name for CZ. Nearly all of the skull-crucible plants used to grow CZ turn out crystals in the half-inch by three-inch size range. That's adequate for use in cutting the normal range of diamond simulants, but nowhere near big enough for a really large diamond like the Cullinan I. My guess is that the crystal this replica was cut from was grown in Russia. The skull-crucible process was originally developed at the Lebedev Physical Institute in Moscow in 1973, and they are probably one of the few organisations who might have developed equipment capable of producing such a large crystal.'

'How does the skull-crucible process work?' asked Paul.

'The starting material used for producing CZ crystals is zirconia powder. This has a very high melting point — well above two-thousand degrees centigrade — and none of the conventional refractory crucibles are capable of withstanding this high temperature. To overcome the problem, the Russian scientists invented a new type of container which consists of an arrangement of water-cooled pipes. The zirconia powder is packed into this and melted by means of radio-frequency induction heating. Because the powder is only electrically conductive in its molten state, the process is started off by inserting a piece of zirconium metal into the powder. The outer circumference of the powder is kept below melting point by the water-cooled container and forms its own high-temperature crucible.'

This was clearly all too much for Steven. 'You said CZ was actually cubic zirconium oxide — where does the cubic bit come in?'

Jeffrey smiled. 'Diamond has a cubic crystal structure, but zirconium oxide is only stable in its cubic form when molten. When it solidifies it becomes monoclinic in structure and opaque — two things which would not make it a good diamond simulant. To keep it in its cubic and transparent state, a stabilizer is mixed in with the source material before heating. That's why it's called cubic zirconium oxide.'

Steven massaged an earlobe. 'I'll take your word for that. The main thing that interests me is the Russian connection. But what would really help us is the name of a cutter who specialises in producing replicas of famous diamonds in CZ.'

Jeffrey shrugged his shoulders. 'Most Cullinan replicas are either moulded from glass or at best are cut from rock crystal.'

He paused and thought for a moment. 'There is, however, one cutter I know who markets sets of replicas of the famous diamonds of the world, and who sometimes uses CZ for some of the smaller stones. It's possible that this replica could also have been cut by him. He's basically a one-man business with a lapidary workshop in Idar-Oberstein — that's the diamond and coloured stone centre in southern Germany. It's also the location of the German Gemmological Association.'

Bryan Raleigh had remained silent during all the technical talk, but now suddenly came to life. 'That sounds like a valuable lead. Can you give us the man's name and address?'

Jeffrey nodded and pulled a battered old filofax from his pocket. He thumbed through its dog-eared pages and finally found what he was searching for. 'Here it is,' he exclaimed triumphantly. 'Rudolph Berger, No.12 Ezenichstrasse, Idar-Oberstein, Germany.'

Paul patted Jeffrey on the back. 'Thanks for your help. That may be the breakthrough we've been looking for.'

After Jeffrey Hamilton had left, Bryan got up and began pacing up and down the limited space of Paul's office. 'I know the crown jewellers have been removed from the frame, but there's another angle we should check out. Within the group of ten wardens who had access to the crown jewels on the evening of the Tower raid, one man had joined the staff only three months previously. His name is George Freeman. I've done a check on him and found he'd retired from the police on pension in 1991. However, in 1995, he left his job as warden on the grounds of ill health. As soon as I heard the news about the Cullinan yesterday I had one of my men visit him on the pretext of doing a survey of police pensioners. If he's a suspect, he doesn't appear to be living extravagantly, but my man did notice betting slips and racing papers on a desk in his lounge.'

Paul nodded. 'I think we'll check him out in more detail. It's just possible he could have a few expensive hobbies, or a skeleton in his closet, despite his excellent police record.' He turned to Steven. 'Get his address from Bryan and pay him a visit.'

* * *

That evening, when Paul and Stephanie returned to their flat in Prince Albert Road, their seventeen-year-old son Jason was in the kitchen. He had already fried himself a generous quantity of bacon, eggs and chips and was busy washing it down with a mug of tea.

Paul sat down beside him at the kitchen table. 'How's the course going?'

'Not bad. The electronic theory is a bit more advanced than the stuff we did in the sixth form — it's the applied maths I'm finding a bit of a grind.'

Jason was taking a degree course in electronic engineering at Regent Street Technical College. 'I still think with your A levels you should have applied for a place at a university,' commented Paul.

Jason shook his head. 'Three years at university would have bored me rigid — this way I get work experience on day release with local companies.'

'Well, it was your choice, so I hope it works out for you.'

Jason finished his tea and got up. 'I'll see how it goes this year. If I do well it's possible one of the companies may sponsor my final year.'

'Are you going out tonight?' asked Paul.

'Yes, I've got tickets for that new space musical, "Aspects of Time".'

'You said tickets. Are you taking someone?'

Jason winked at him. 'It's a tasty dish from my class — but don't tell mother.'

'A budding female engineer could be an asset. If you bring her back here afterwards, just keep the noise level down.'

Stephanie walked into the kitchen as Jason was leaving.

'Night, mum. Don't wait up for me,' He grabbed his coat and shot out the door.

Stephanie collected up the dirty dishes and stacked them in the dish washer. 'Was that our son who just left?' she asked.

'He's off to see a new musical — I've warned him to be quiet when he comes in.' Paul walked across to Stephanie and took her in his arms. 'You look a bit weary. Why don't we have a glass of wine and then go out for a meal tonight — I don't see why Jason should have all the fun.'

Stephanie kissed him. 'Now you're talking — that's just the

antidote I need after a hard day at the office. The pace always hots up before the Sights. And how was your day?'

Paul grimaced. 'Not bad. After Sir James came back from his meeting yesterday at number ten he was in something of a dither. But things have calmed down a bit now.'

'What was that meeting all about? He sent me out on an errand just before you and Steven arrived.' Paul pulled her closer. 'It's all a bit hush, hush, but you've had to keep secrets before so just listen to this.' He told her briefly about the missing Cullinan I, and of their suspicions that it was substituted during the attack on the Tower.

Stephanie listened carefully until he had finished. 'If the diamond was stolen by the gang, why wasn't it recovered from one of the bodies?' she asked.

'After the raid, the crown jewels were checked, and nothing appeared to be missing. Even so, a thorough search was made of the bodies when they were recovered from the Thames the following day.'

'What about the wreckage from the helicopter?'

'That was salvaged and thoroughly checked out also.' Stephanie considered this. 'But as you've just said, the Crown Jewels appeared to be intact, so no one was actually looking for a large diamond.'

Paul glanced at her in surprise. 'I think you're on to something. If the Cullinan was in the helicopter when it blew up, it could still be lying in the mud at the bottom of the river. I'll phone Bryan Raleigh first thing tomorrow. That whole stretch of the river will have to be dredged.'

* * *

Leo Vandam picked up the phone in his Cape Town 'Eagles Nest' headquarters. 'Yes, who is it?'

'Hallo, Leo, it's George Freeman.'

Leo signalled for Clive Drake to pick up the extension. 'I told you never to call me here.'

'Sorry, Leo. I thought you should know I had a rather strange visit from a plain clothes copper. He said he was checking up on police pensioners. I telephoned another retired colleague of mine in the area. He hadn't been visited.'

'There's no reason for you to be concerned, George. The business deal we had was five years ago — keep a low profile, and live normally.'

'OK, Leo, but I thought you should know.'

Leo put down his handset. He turned and glared at Clive Drake. 'It seems you left some unfinished business in London. Now that we've got the Brazilian problem to sort out, I can't afford the possibility of another potential leak. Just make sure of Freeman's silence.'

Clive's eyes glinted behind his glasses. 'Leave it to me, Leo. I know the ideal man to plug a leak.' He smiled coldly and dialled a London number.

CHAPTER 14

LONDON
Saturday 11 September, 1999

When Paul spoke to Bryan Raleigh on the telephone that morning, he felt certain the mystery of 'The Phantom Diamond' was about to be solved.

'I think the stone could be buried in the silt at the bottom of the Thames — can you check this out as a possibility?' he asked Bryan.

'Bloody hell,' exclaimed Bryan. 'You could just be right. I'll get a team of divers on to it right away.'

He paused. 'I'll also arrange for a couple of sand dredgers to be brought down from London Docks. We can set up a sieve on each vessel and dump the waste overboard.'

'One other thing, Bryan, you'd better circulate a cover story to account for all the activity — it's bound to attract a lot of interest from Joe public.'

'No problem. We'll say there's the possibility of a war-time thousand-pounder sitting somewhere at the bottom of the river. That'll give us a good reason to restrict the river traffic for a day or two.'

'Good idea. When you've got the search underway, I'll come down and take a look.'

* * *

By the following morning a team of six divers and the two dredgers were on station a few hundred yards upstream from Tower Bridge. The divers were being used to control the positions of the suction hoses of the two big dredgers as the vessels moved slowly in tandem over a two-hundred yard stretch of the river. The hoses were suspended from the bows of the dredgers, and after the slurry was sucked up from the bed of the river and passed through large 10mm mesh screens, it was pumped back into the river from the rear of the vessels. Large objects too big for the suction hoses were recovered with a wire dredging net which was checked and emptied after each run.

When Paul visited the site the next day he was impressed with the way it had been organised. 'This looks rather like the off-shore diamond recovery methods used along the Namibian coast,' he commented to Bryan.

'Yes, if you ignore the smell and the rows of lunchtime spectators on both sides of the embankment,' agreed Bryan.

The results, after four full days of intensive work, were disappointing to say the least. Objects recovered from the river's ancient bed included several rusty prams, hundreds of beer bottles and tins, five hand guns, two of which were later traced back to armed robberies, three decomposed cats, a few more fragments of the Chinook helicopter, and a denture which one of the lunchtime onlookers claimed he lost overboard during an alcoholic river cruise the previous Christmas. The most valuable articles recovered from the silt were two wedding rings and a diamond engagement ring.

Noel Lancaster, the Police Commissioner, visited the site on the fourth day of dredging and had a few terse words to say to DCI Raleigh concerning the expense of the operation. That evening the search was called off, and the 'Phantom Diamond' was back at the top of the missing list again.

* * *

During the second day of the dredging operation on the Monday, Steven paid a visit to George Freeman's home in the London suburb of Bromley. He parked his car at the roadside and walked up the path to the front door. The semi-detached house looked in good decorative condition, and the small front garden was neat and ablaze with full-blown autumn roses. He rang the front door bell, but there was no answer. After a few minutes the door of the other half of the semi opened and a young woman appeared. 'Are you looking for Mr Freeman?' she asked. Steven nodded. 'Do you know when he'll be back?'

'I'm afraid he's in hospital. There was a gas leak in his kitchen. It seems the oven blew up when he tried to light it.'

'When did this happen?'

'Yesterday evening. I heard this big bang, and dialled 999 — thought the IRA were at it again. He looked in a bad way when they carried him out to the ambulance.' The woman smiled at Steven. 'You a friend of his, then?'

'Sort of. We were both in the Metropolitan Police. I was asked to deliver some pension documents to him.'

'They took him to Bromley General in Lownds Avenue — it's just off Market Square.' Steven thanked the woman and walked back to his car.

When he arrived at the hospital, he went straight to the enquiry desk. 'I understand Mr George Freeman was admitted here yesterday. Can you tell me how he's getting on?'

The girl behind the desk looked up at him. 'Are you a relative?'

Steven shook his head. 'No, I'm a police colleague — I've got some important papers for him to sign. Is he well enough for me to see him?'

'I'm very sorry, he died shortly after they brought him in. His brother and sister were here earlier. If you ask to see the matron she can put you in touch with them.'

'Thanks for your help. I'll tell the personnel people to do that.' Steven walked thoughtfully back to his car. 'Another convenient death,' he muttered. 'That makes ten with the helicopter explosion.'

***

The day following the suspension of the dredging operation, Paul and Steven were in DCI Bryan Raleigh's office at New Scotland Yard discussing the current state of their investigations. Bryan had perched himself on the corner of his desk, his hands thrust deep into the pockets of his knitted cardigan.

'Let me summarise where we've got to so far,' he said. 'We know our ex-KGB friend Leo Vandam is an art dealer based in

Cape Town. We also know one of his KGB operatives took part in the theft of the Golconda d'Or in Sydney back in 1980. But despite this, and the fact that the man who telephoned and alerted us to the raid on the Tower had a South African accent, we have no hard evidence linking Leo to the substitution of the Cullinan I.'

'Did you find out anything suspicious about George Freeman's death,' asked Steven. 'Until a few days ago he was the only remaining live suspect on our list.'

'Yes, the CID are pretty certain his death wasn't an accident. The cooker was virtually destroyed by the explosion, but among the remains they found a charred battery and a piece of printed circuit board. The cooker's metal taps were still intact — they were all turned hard on.'

'So what's the verdict?' asked Paul.

'They're pretty certain that George Freeman was murdered. A window at the rear of the house had been forced, and they suspect the intruder knew of the man's movements and had broken in a few hours before he was expected home. Their guess is that the intruder turned the gas taps on, and left a proximity-operated igniter somewhere in the kitchen.'

Steven raked his fingers through his hair. 'So, by implication, it looks as if George Freeman, who was engaged as a warden three months before the raid on the Tower, was the man on the inside. Not only would he have been able to keep the mastermind behind the raid informed of the security and transfer arrangements, but it's feasible he was also the means of bringing out the diamond.'

'It's also significant that he was murdered a few days after one of my men called on him. No doubt somebody thought we were getting too close for comfort, and decided to silence him,' said Bryan

'I'm beginning to believe that's what happened,' agreed Paul. 'The whole object of the raid was to steal the Cullinan I, and then make us think the raid was a failure. The anonymous phone call warning us of the raid was an essential part of the plan. It was important that the raid was interrupted by the arrival of the SAS. The substitution of the CZ replica for the Cullinan was all part of the illusion. Even if this had been discovered early on, no doubt someone was waiting at Freeman's home that night to collect the diamond and spirit it out of the country.'

'If that's the way it happened, the destruction of the helicopter and all those on board was a pretty callous act,' commented Steven.

'And one which I'm sure Leo would have been capable of,' added Paul. 'As they say, dead men tell no tales.' He pulled the CZ replica out of his pocket. 'This is now our one remaining piece of evidence. I think it's time Steven and I paid a visit to the lapidary in Idar-Oberstein who specialises in these models. If it's not one of his, he may know who made it.'

CHAPTER 15

IDAR-OBERSTEIN
Monday 20 September, 1999

Paul and Steven had taken the early morning flight from Heathrow to Luxemburg, and then hired a car and driven north-east into Germany and on to Trier. From there they followed the winding course of the Mosel as it flowed between the gently sloping contours of its vineyard-covered banks until they came to the old town of Bernkastel-Kues straddling the river. Then they turned south-east and headed through pine-scented forests to Idar-Oberstein.

The gem industry sited in and around the twin town of Idar-Oberstein came into being in Roman times with the discovery of an abundant supply of agate and other quartz minerals among the rocks of the surrounding hillsides. In those days the towns of Idar and Oberstein were separate entities linked only by a narrow road and the river Nahe, a tributary of the Rhine. Over several hundred years, the boundaries of the two towns slowly merged, although there remained some of the traditional rivalry that had always existed between the inhabitants of the two areas.

The thriving gem industry of Idar-Oberstein began to decline in the nineteenth century when local sources of agate became worked out. The industry was only saved from extinction when several enterprising Idar lapidaries emigrated to Brazil in search of an alternative supply of rough gem material. In 1827 they discovered great quantities of agate and quartz gems lying on and just beneath the surface of Rio Grande de Sol. When the news reached Idar, more gem workers emigrated over the following years, and began to send back a great variety of high quality gemstones.

One of these émigrés was the great grandfather of lapidary

Rudolph Berger, whose home and workshop were located in Ezenichstrasse, at the north-western end of Idar. When Paul and Steven reached the outskirts of the town in the early afternoon, Paul stopped and got out of the car to ask directions at a petrol station.

'Bitte, ich wunsche Rudolph Berger nach zwolf Eisstrasse besuchen. Konnen Sie mir hilfen?' he asked the attendant.

'Ah, you must be Dutch — I think you mean Ezenichstrasse,' the man replied. 'Herr Berger's house is fifty metres ahead on the right.' He pointed to a two-storey granite-faced house standing back from the road.

Paul thanked the man and got back into the car. 'So much for your school German,' grinned Steven. 'Let's hope friend Rudolph also speaks English.'

Paul drove down the road and parked outside the house. The long building had two doorways. Paul rang the bell on the one with the sign 'Buro — R. Berger, Schleifer.' After a few seconds the door was opened by a boy in his early teens.

'Good day — ich mochte mit Herr Berger sprechen, bitte.'

'Hallo, my name is Karl — I'll call my father.'

Steven laughed. 'You've struck lucky again.'

Rudolph Berger was a short rotund man in his mid forties. He was in shirt sleeves and was wearing a leather apron over a pair of grubby jeans. 'Please to excuse my working clothes,' he said in halting English. He wiped his hands on some cotton waste and shook hands with Paul and Steven. 'Please excuse also my poor English. My son Karl — he speak it better. Now, you wish talk with me?'

'My name is Paul Remington, and this is my colleague Steven Heming. We are from the Diamond Syndicate in London. I understand you make replicas of famous diamonds.'

'Yes — I show you. Please come into office.' He led them into a small room containing an oak roll-top desk, a table and two glass-fronted display cabinets. A net-curtained window looked out on the road, and in front of it there was a photocopier sitting on a metal filing cabinet. In one of the display cabinets Paul could see rows of diamond models mounted on perspex stands.

'Let me show you number one selling line.' Rudolph Berger

nodded to his son who took an embossed red leather case out of a drawer in the desk and laid it on the table. Rudolph opened the case lovingly. 'Here are twenty-one models of world famous large diamonds. You see — each one is labelled with name and weight of stone.'

Steven inspected the models lying in the blue satin-lined compartments of the case. 'What are the replicas made of?'

Rudolph picked up the largest one labelled 'Cullinan I — 530.2 carats'. 'With colourless diamond like this one, model is made from quartz. For coloured diamonds I use...' he hesitated, searching for the right word and turned to his son for help.

Karl took a blue-coloured stone labelled 'Hope diamond — 45.52 carat' from the case. 'For models of coloured diamonds like this one, my father uses synthetic corundum, or spinel, of the correct colour.'

Paul took the quartz model from Rudolph and inspected it. 'Have you ever made a model of the Cullinan I in CZ?'

Rudolph smiled. 'Nur einmal — only once.' He looked pleadingly at his son again.

'My father finds it difficult to get a large enough crystal of CZ for such a big stone,' said Karl. 'He normally uses flawless pieces of quartz from Brazil.'

Paul pulled his CZ replica of the Cullinan I from his pocket and compared it with the quartz model. Steven looked over his shoulder. 'I can see why it fooled the crown jewellers,' he murmured. 'It makes the quartz version look lifeless.'

Paul handed his replica to Rudolph. 'This is a CZ model — can you tell me if you made this one?'

Rudolph took the replica from Paul and held it up against the light. 'I think so — come with me in my workshop and I will show you.'

They all followed him into a large room at the back of the building. Two vertical grindstones, each four feet in diameter, dominated the room. Around the walls were shelves containing dishes and pots of grinding and polishing compounds. Between the shelves were boards from which hung dozens of metal plates pierced with holes of various shapes.

Rudolph picked up a steel rule and laid it edge downwards

across the large table facet of the CZ replica. He held the stone and rule up to the fluorescent light suspended from the ceiling, and beckoned Paul to his side. 'Edge of metal rule is flat against facet — it touch the stone at each end, but see — a little light comes through the middle.'

Paul took the rule and the stone and squinted along the facet as Rudolph had done. 'Yes, I can see the light coming under the rule in the centre of the facet — but what does that prove?'

'It means was made by me. I first cut profile of stone from CZ crystal. I use metal template to get shape.' He pointed to the metal plates hanging from the boards on the wall. 'Then I facet stone on these big grindstones. But result is facet has very slight curve — it not flat. That is why light escape from centre of metal rule. Other schleifers use flat polishing lap, but this slower than my way.'

Paul turned to Karl. 'Could you please ask your father who he made this CZ model for?'

Karl held a brief conversation with Rudolph, and turned back to Paul. 'He will look it up in his account book — it was several years ago.'

While Rudolph searched through his account books, Paul chatted to his son. 'I think we will stay the night in Idar-Oberstein — can you recommend a good hotel.'

'You must stay in the Swan,' answered the boy. 'It's only a few hundred metres from here, and they cook the best *spiesbraten* in Idar.'

'What is spiesbraten?' asked Steven who was beginning to feel hungry.

'It's a local speciality. A thick piece of beef or pork, soaked in a special sauce, and cooked on a spit over a charcoal fire. You must try it tonight.'

'Sounds great. Is there anything else we should sample while we're here?'

'There are two famous mineral museums, an old one in Oberstein, and a modern one in the Diamond Bourse building here in Idar. You can also visit the old gem mine at Steinkaulenberg in the mountains, and of course there is the Deutsche Gemmologische Gesellschaft Centrum, that's the German Gem

Association headquarters and laboratories not far from the Bourse.'

At this point, Rudolph Berger looked up from his account books and unclipped a sheet of paper. 'I find it. Here is order for CZ copy.' He handed the paper to Paul and pointed to a note at the bottom of the sheet. 'You see. CZ crystals sent with order for Cullinan I model on October 21, 1993.'

Paul took the order from Rudolph and read out the name of the company on the heading. 'L. Vandam, Antiques, PO Box 3098, Cape Town 8000, Republic of South Africa.'

'Bingo,' exclaimed Steven. 'We've got the bastard!'

'You mustn't mind my friend — he gets rather excited sometimes,' apologised Paul. 'Can I please have a photocopy of this order?'

Rudolph nodded. He took the sheet of paper from Paul and pointed to the door. They followed him back into his office and waited while he made a copy and gave it to Paul.

Rudolph held up his hand. 'There is more I must show you.' He walked across to one of the display cabinets and lifted out a box. He removed the lid from the box and took out a colourless crystal five inches long by three and a half inches in diameter, its fluted lustrous surfaces glistening in the fluorescent light. 'This is second of two crystals sent me with order - in case I make mistake with first.' He handed Paul a piece of crumpled paper. 'Crystals were wrapped in this.'

Paul took the crumpled piece of brown paper and smoothed it out. At one end there was a grubby label. Across the label were printed three words in the Russian cyrillic script.

'Can you translate this for me, Rudolph?' asked Paul.

Rudolph took back the paper. 'Yes — I know Russian script. It says Lebedev Physical Institute.'

At that moment a middle-aged woman entered the room carrying a tray of small glasses and a bottle. Rudolph took the tray from her and laid it on the table. 'This is my frau — my wife. Her name is Lisle, but her English less good than me!'

Lisle smiled shyly at Paul and Steven. 'I see my man has guests,' she said. 'So I bring you drinks.'

'Es freut mich, Sie zu treffen, Frau Berger.' Paul turned to

Karl. 'And please tell your father we are very much in his debt. What he has just told us has been of great help. We would like to invite you all to join us in a spiesbraten at the Swan tonight. Then you can help us further by recommending some of your local wine.'

While Karl passed on the invitation to his father, Lisle poured them all a glass of schnapps.

Rudolph Berger raised his glass in a toast. 'Prosit und viel Gluck!'

Karl handed Paul a tourist guide to Idar-Oberstein. 'It is still not late. If you like I can take you to your hotel, and then show you some of town's attractions.'

'I would like that, Karl.' Paul winked at Steven. 'After what we learned today, this may be our last chance for a few hours of rest and relaxation. I have a gut feeling the next trip will be to Cape Town!'

CHAPTER 16

LONDON
Tuesday 21 September, 1999

Paul handed DCI Bryan Raleigh the photocopy of Leo Vandam's order for the CZ model of the Cullinan I. It was the afternoon of Paul's return from Germany, and he was sitting in Bryan's office at New Scotland Yard.

'Rudolph Berger, the German lapidary we visited in Idar-Oberstein, positively identified the replica of the Cullinan as his work,' Paul explained. 'Berger specialises in making models of the world's famous diamonds, but unlike the other lapidaries in this line of work, he uses a different polishing technique. As this was the only one he's ever made out of CZ, it was then simply a matter of finding out who had ordered the replica. When he looked up the order in his accounts book he found it was dated October 21, 1993. He told me the finished CZ model was sent by registered post to Cape Town a month later. The raid on the Tower took place on February 6 the following year, so the dates fit.'

Bryan read the letter heading on the photocopy. 'So we've finally got some hard evidence on our ex-KGB colonel.'

Paul nodded. 'I think the time is ripe for us to visit Cape Town. Can you get away for a few days?'

Bryan re-read the photocopy. Then he swivelled his chair around and gazed out of the window. The early promise of an Indian summer had faded, and a late autumn had turned into an early winter with plummeting temperatures. A squall of rain suddenly rattled against the glass of the window and momentarily hid his view of the grey river scene.

He turned back to face Paul and grinned. 'In answer to your question — no problem. I can't think of a better reason to escape from all this. Anyway, operation The Phantom Diamond has been given top priority by my bosses. We've already used up nearly two weeks of the five months we had at the start of this investigation, and they're getting agitated.'

'I know the feeling. Sir James has got a big two-year calender on the wall of his office, and he's crossing off the days to the coronation on Thursday 16 March. We've started calling it coronary day, which is what he'll have if we don't come up with the goods before then.'

Bryan stifled a laugh. 'Now to be serious for a moment. Providing you've no objection, I suggest we take a direct flight to Cape Town tomorrow evening. That will give us both time to sort out a few things at the office first. In the meanwhile, I'll talk to the Diamond and Gold branch of the South African Police in Cape Town, and warn them we're coming. Will you be taking Steven Heming along?'

'He's not going to like it, but the answer is no. There are a few things going on in our own backyard at the moment, and I need him in London as an anchor man.' Paul went to his brief case and took out the CZ replica of the Cullinan. 'I'll take this with me to South Africa — I've a strange feeling it might come in handy.'

* * *

That evening Paul broke the news to Stephanie that he would be leaving for Cape Town the next day. 'I'll put Sir James in the picture tomorrow morning — it should cheer him up to hear we're making some progress at last. He was a bit morose when we drew a blank with the dredging operation.'

Stephanie pouted. 'I might have guessed you'd find an excuse to get away from this bloody awful weather.' She handed him an airmail letter. 'This was in our mailbox when I got home this evening.'

Paul took the letter out of its envelope and read it. 'So, Christine, Mike and Melanie are in Cape Town on holiday at the moment — that's a coincidence.'

'You're right Paul — and it gives me a great idea. What if I joined you, and flew out to Cape Town. I've still got a week of my leave to use up.'

Before Paul could answer, Jason bounded into the room. 'I heard that — I hope you weren't planning to sneak off to the sun and leave me behind all on my own?'

Paul looked up in alarm. 'Now take it easy the two of you. I'm going to South Africa with DCI Raleigh to do a job of work…'

'We promise not to get in your way,' interrupted Stephanie. She winked at Jason. 'And think of the money you'll save in not having to make those long phone calls to us each evening from Cape Town.'

'Dad, did I hear you say that Melanie is in Cape Town too?' Jason tried to make his question sound casual.

Paul shook his head in resignation. He handed the airmail letter to Jason. 'I've decided to leave Steven behind in London as backup — he'll be well pleased when he hears I'm taking you lot with me on a jolly.'

Stephanie was beginning to have second thoughts about Jason's participation in her scheme. 'What about your studies at the Regent Street College?' she asked.

Jason looked up from the letter. 'If Melanie can take three weeks off from university, I don't see why I shouldn't do the same. I can easily miss the next period of work experience. I'll simply pick up the course again in October.'

'That's settled then,' announced Stephanie. She walked across to Paul and kissed him. 'I'll just have to tell Sir James I can't trust you on your own in South Africa. After all, that was the real reason the company insisted on sending wives out with their husbands when they went overseas for any length of time.'

'Sir James is not going to be pleased with you giving such a short notice,' countered Paul. 'He likes to brood about any change in his routine for at least a month.'

'I'll arrange for your giggly secretary Debbie to take care of him. He appreciates me all the more when he has to do without me for a few days.' Stephanie took the letter back from Jason whose eyes had taken on a dreamy look at the prospect of a reunion with Melanie. She scanned the letter again. 'Christine has written on hotel notepaper — they're staying at the Mount Nelson. I'll phone her right away and ask her to make a reservation for us all in the same hotel. I'm sure your expenses will cover the bill, darling. Then I'll start packing our cases.'

Paul turned to Jason and sighed. 'Thanks a lot for your support — I was quite looking forward to a few peaceful days in the sun.'

Stephanie laughed. 'Now cheer up — you would soon have missed my tender loving care, particularly at night. Tomorrow you can ask your nice travel girl to book two extra tickets on the evening flight to Cape Town. Oh yes, and just make sure Bryan Raleigh wears some clothes suitable for the Cape summer, I don't want him arriving at London Airport in that dreadful old cardigan.'

CHAPTER 17

LONDON — CAPE TOWN
Thursday 23 September, 1999

The giant five-hundred seater Boeing 777 to Cape Town was fully booked, but the Syndicate's travel department had managed to get Stephanie and Jason standby seats in economy class. Paul and Bryan Raleigh had seats in business class, and in honour of the occasion, Bryan had abandoned his cardigan and jeans, and was resplendent in a white shirt, light-weight cream jacket and blue linen slacks. After the evening meal, Bryan volunteered to swap seats with Stephanie so that she could be with Paul.

Both Bryan and Jason had seen the film that was being screened after the dinner, and the young man took the opportunity to quiz Bryan about his work in the Art and Antiques Investigation Squad at the Yard.

'It's not as exciting as it sounds.' explained Bryan. 'Most of my time is spent in updating computer records so we can keep tabs on who owns what. When artifacts are stolen, this makes it possible to identify and return them if, for example, they re-appear in auction catalogues.'

Jason sounded disappointed. 'But don't you ever get involved in raids and arrests?'

'Very rarely. When we get a positive ID on a stolen item, the main CID section does the physical bit. Our job is the investigation part. We have our paid informers, and we keep track of all known fences and art dealers. For example, the reason Paul and I are going to Cape Town is to check on a dealer called Vandam.'

'I've heard about him from my father. He sounds a bit of a character.'

'Yes, I managed to get the South African Police file on him faxed to me via Interpol. It makes interesting reading. His background in the army and the KGB makes him sound like a real tough cookie, but he's also quite a cultural guy, with an interest in Russian classical composers. Prokofiev seems to be his favourite. Information like that, particularly about people in the art world, is our stock-in-trade. These days it's all computer-based and linked worldwide via Interpol and the Internet.' Bryan switched off his reading light. 'I expect you're well clued up yourself on computers and software?'

'I'm taking a degree-level course in electronics. As far as computers go, I just use them for wordprocessing my notes and homework assignments, although later on the course does cover CAD, and in particular computer-aided design of integrated circuits. Melanie, that's Mike and Christine's daughter who we'll be meeting in Cape Town tomorrow, is taking computer science at Wits University in Jo'burg. She's a whizz kid on the PC keyboard. When we visited them over Christmas last year, she let slip she was a member of a secret hackers group at the university — but that's strictly off the record. She'd kill me if her parents got to know.'

Bryan laughed. 'As a copper I'm appalled — but don't worry, her secret is safe with me. I look forward to meeting this Melanie of yours. Now I suggest we get our heads down. Tomorrow promises to be a full day.'

* * *

Next morning, Mike, Christine and daughter Melanie were waiting for them as they emerged from the customs hall in Cape Town's international airport.

Christine hugged Stephanie. 'Lovely to see you again — it's been far too long since your Christmas visit.'

Paul introduced Bryan Raleigh to Mike and family, while Jason and Melanie greeted each other politely and cooly as if they were meeting for the first time.

Paul took Mike on one side. 'Bryan has been in touch with the Diamond and Gold Branch of the SAP, and we've got an appointment to meet one of their senior officers in Cape Town's Sea Point headquarters this afternoon.' He grimaced and lowered his voice.

'Looking at our wives and children, you'd never guess the two of us were here on official business.'

Mike raked a hand through his curly brown hair. 'I'll bear it in mind. Now let's sort out the transport.'

Paul pulled a book of car vouchers from his wallet. 'I've arranged a hire car for Bryan and myself. If you can squeeze Stephanie and Jason in your car, Mike, we'll take all the luggage in the hire car and follow you into town.'

Jason was secretly pleased to find himself alongside Melanie in her father's Volvo estate, and during the thirty-minute journey from the airport the slightly strained atmosphere between them began to dissolve. 'Wow,' he exclaimed, momentarily distracted from his conversation with her by the famous mountain range of Devil's Peak, Table Mountain, Lion's Head and Signal Hill. 'Now that view really is something!'

Christine turned round to speak to Stephanie. 'Mike and I always love our first glimpse of Cape Town and the mountain when we drive in from the airport.' She pointed at the seaward end of the city spread out below them. 'Straight ahead you can see the Nico Malan Opera House and Theatre — the long building is the Civic Centre. Beyond that is the Victoria and Alfred Waterfront. On the left where those trees are is the Parliament building, and to the left of that you can just see the pink walls of the Mount Nelson Hotel where we're all staying.'

Melanie nudged Jason. 'Our rooms are next to each other,' she whispered.

Mike signalled a left turn off the N2 and checked in his mirror to see that Paul and Bryan were following him. He drove past the hexagonal ramparts of Cape Town's squat castle, and then made another left turn. A few minutes later they drove under the white Prince of Wales archway and cruised up the Mount Nelson Hotel's palm-fringed driveway to a rambling colonial-style pink edifice

When they drew up at the hotel entrance, Jason sighed. 'This place is really impressive, but I'm not sure I like the colour — it's so pink.' He ducked Melanie's fist and laughed. 'OK, I expect I'll get used to it with your help.'

* * *

That afternoon, Paul and Bryan visited the police headquarters at the junction of Regent and Main in the Sea Point area of Cape Town. At the enquiry desk, Bryan spoke to the young female duty officer. 'Excuse me, miss. My name is Bryan Raleigh from Scotland Yard, London. I and my colleague Paul Remington have an appointment with your Inspector Duuren of the Diamond and Gold Branch.'

The young girl was wearing a crisply-ironed khaki-coloured blouse and dark brown skirt. 'I'll let Inspector Duuren know you here.' She made a brief telephone call and then nodded to the two men. 'The inspector will see you right away.' She pointed to the corridor. 'He's in room six on the right.'

When they entered the sparsely furnished room, a thick-set man in his mid fifties with sun-reddened skin and close-cropped white hair was opening a window. He turned and greeted them in a strong Afrikaans accent. 'My name is Duuren — sorry about the temperature in here. The sun is on this side of the building in the afternoon. But still, I expect that is a welcome change from your country's climate.'

The man's accent reminded Bryan that not all Afrikaners were completely at ease with the English language. 'Yes,' he agreed. 'When we spoke together on the phone two days ago the temperature in London was only five degrees centigrade. Now let me introduce you to my colleague Paul Remington from the Diamond Syndicate in London.'

The inspector nodded and shook hands with Paul, and then indicated for them to use the chairs which had been set out around a table near the window.

'I want to thank you for agreeing to see us,' continued Bryan. 'When we spoke on the phone I was only able to give you a brief idea of the reason for our visit to Cape Town.'

Inspector Duuren cleared his throat. 'I understand you are dealing with a very sensitive matter. For this the telephone may not be safe. You also mentioned a Mr Vandam of Clifton.'

Bryan nodded and indicated for Paul to take up the story. 'You probably know that our Queen Elizabeth is giving up the throne at the end of this year, and that she will be succeeded by Prince William her grandson.'

'Yes, I have heard of this, Mr Remington.'

'The coronation of King William is planned for March 16 of next year. However, it has recently been discovered that the large diamond in the royal sceptre, which plays a major part in the coronation ceremony, has been stolen and replaced by an imitation.'

Inspector Duuren's face registered astonishment. 'You telling me the Cullinan I, which was cut from the big stone President Paul Kruger presented to your King Edward seventh, is stolen?'

Paul nodded. 'That's right, Inspector Duuren. We believe it happened nearly five years ago when there was an armed raid on the Tower of London.'

'I remember reading that — but the reports said the raid had failed.'

'That's what everyone thought,' agreed Bryan. 'But when the crown jewels were being cleaned last month in preparation for the coronation, the Cullinan diamond was found to be a CZ copy. Made from CZ, the replica was of course a very convincing substitute. You can see now why we wish to keep this affair secret. The theft is known to only a few people in the UK, and we use the code name Phantom Diamond when we discuss it on the phone or by fax. Our objective is to recover the diamond and replace it in the royal sceptre before the coronation takes place. This is the only way we can avoid a national scandal.'

'That is a most remarkable situation,' said Inspector Duuren, shaking his head. 'But it does not explain why you are here.'

Bryan extracted a piece of paper from his wallet and unfolded it. 'This is a photocopy of an order to make a replica of the Cullinan I. It was sent to a lapidary in Germany. We have recently shown this man the CZ replica that was found in the royal sceptre, and he has confirmed it is the same stone he made against this order.' Bryan handed the photocopy to the inspector. 'You will see that the order came from L. Vandam, Antique Dealers, who have their base here in Clifton, just a mile or two from where we sit.'

Inspector Duuren blew out his cheeks. 'I know this man Vandam. He came to South Africa from Moscow in 1990 with several million rand. We issued him with a probationary five-year residence permit, and when that expired, he was given a ten-year one. Although we were suspicious of his background at the beginning, he has caused no trouble here in Cape Town.'

Bryant handed Inspector Duuren a second photocopy. 'This is a photofit picture of a man who was involved in the theft of a large yellow diamond in Sydney, Australia in 1980. He has been identified as an ex-KGB operative. As I'm sure you're aware, before Vandam changed his name he was Leo Vessovsky, head of the KGB. We suspect he was behind the theft in Sydney ten years before he left Russia. The proceeds were probably part of the money he brought with him to South Africa.'

Inspector Duuren looked uncomfortable. 'Yes, our intelligence service warned us of Mr Vandam's former army and KGB careers. But as I said, he has caused us no problems. In those days, you must understand, we welcomed business men who brought large amounts of hard currency into our country.'

Bryan glanced at Paul and raised his eyebrows. He retrieved the two photocopies and laid them side-by-side on the table. 'Inspector Duuren, we were hoping for your co-operation in obtaining more evidence linking Vandam, as he now calls himself, to the substitution of the Cullinan.'

'What level of co-operation are you asking?'

'First of all, can you show us a recent photo of Vandam.'

Inspector Duuren opened a folder on the table and handed Bryan a photograph. 'This is an enlargement of his passport photograph.'

Bryan passed the photograph to Paul. 'He looks like a bloated Yul Brunner.'

Paul studied Vandam's face for a few seconds. 'As my colleague mentioned, what we badly need now is more evidence. Can you have a search warrant issued, and organise a raid on his premises?'

'My dear Mr Remington, I would need more than your suspicions and these two pieces of paper to obtain a search warrant. It seems you have nothing so far but circumstantial evidence. In this new rainbow democracy of ours, I need more than that. In the old apartheid days things were rather different. Come back to me with something more concrete and I will be happy to help you. In the meanwhile, enjoy your visit to Cape Town.'

Inspector Duuren stood up and shook hands with both men. 'I'm sorry I can't help you further.' He bowed to them curtly in dismissal, and ushered them out of the room.

Outside the Police Headquarters, Paul looked at Bryan in dismay. 'I hadn't expected that. Maybe it's money talking. Let's go back to the Mount Nelson and lick our wounds.'

* * *

When they arrived at the hotel, Mike was waiting for them with Christine and Stephanie.

'How did your meeting go,' asked Mike.

'It was a bit of a non event,' answered Bryan. 'We basically got nowhere — but we'll discuss it later. Where are the youngsters?'

'Melanie is showing Jason around the Victoria and Alfred Waterfront,' said Christine. 'They said they'd be back in time for dinner. I thought the rest of us could round off the day by going up Signal Hill to see the sun go down and watch the lights of the city come up. We've bought a couple of bottles of wine, and we've borrowed some glasses and a corkscrew from the hotel, so while we're up there we can drink a toast to your first day in Cape Town.'

Mike collected his Volvo estate from the hotel multi-story park, and picked up Bryan, Paul and the two girls at the hotel entrance. He took the Kloof Nek road round the western end of Table Mountain. At the roundabout leading to the lower cable-car station he turned right and began to ascend the tree-lined flank of Lion's Head, a rocky outcrop whose rump formed the conical viewpoint called Signal Hill. As the road twisted and turned, Paul and Stephanie caught glimpses of the city stretched out beneath them against the ever-present backdrop of Table Mountain and Devil's Peak. When they reached the summit of

Signal Hill Mike parked the car, and they sauntered back down the roadway to get a better view of the city and the coastline.

Mike pointed to the busy dock area. 'Melanie and Jason are somewhere down there in the Waterfront development to the left of the main docks. It's got dozens of restaurants and shops, a hotel, a multiple-screen cinema and an aquarium. You can also get a boat trip to Robben Island where Mandela was imprisoned.'

By now the sun was beginning to sink towards the western horizon, so Mike led them back to a picnic area at the top of the hill. They sat round one of the circular stone tables while he uncorked the bottles of wine and filled their glasses. As the setting sun was beginning to tint the clouds on the horizon with pink and golden streaks, Mike raised his glass in a toast. 'Here's to you, Stephanie and Paul, and to your first sunset on Signal Hill.'

When the sun had finally set, they returned to the car and drove a few hundred yards down the hill. Mike pulled to the side of the road for a few minutes so they could enjoy the spectacle of the city's lights. As the dark descended, Stephanie glanced up at Table Mountain. 'Look, Paul,' she whispered. 'The whole face of the mountain is floodlit.'

On the return journey, Mike took them down the other side of Lion's Head to join the coast road. When they came to Clifton, he pointed out Leo Vandam's 'Eagles Nest' headquarters.

'That's quite a secure hideout he's got there,' commented Bryan as he squinted up in the half light at the white-painted two-storey house perched high on the rock face.

* * *

After dinner that evening, Jason joined Mike, Bryan and Paul in a quiet corner of the bar. The conversation between the men dried up as Jason sat down.

'Can I have a beer?' Jason asked his father. Paul nodded moodily, and signalled the waiter. He turned back to Bryan.

'We can talk in front of Jason — he knows the bare facts about the Phantom Diamond substitution.'

The waiter served Jason his beer, and the boy sipped it appreciatively. 'How did things go at your meeting this afternoon?' he asked.

'Not at all well,' answered Bryan. 'The police don't think we've given them enough reason to apply for a search warrant. In the new South Africa they're more sensitive now about civil rights. We suspect that Leo Vandam may have bought himself a degree of police protection.'

Jason brooded on this for a few minutes while he drank his beer. Then an idea came to him. 'Melanie has brought her notebook computer on holiday with her. She showed it to me while you were at your meeting.'

'What are you getting at Jason,' asked his father.

'The notebook has got a built-in modem, so she can send her assignments by electronic mail to Wits University while she's away.'

'So what's that got to do with anything?' asked Mike.

Jason looked uncomfortable and glanced at Bryan.

Bryan frowned. 'I think I can guess what's on Jason's mind. It could be another way of getting some hard evidence against Vandam. Can I tell them about it, Jason?'

'Melanie will kill me, but I suppose it's OK if it helps to nail the Ruskie.'

Bryan turned to Mike. 'Now you mustn't get angry with Melanie. Jason told me in confidence that she's a member of a computer hacking group at Wits. I think Jason believes she's capable of using her computer to gain access to the contents of Leo's machine.'

'That's right,' agreed Jason. 'Why don't we go and ask her if she'll do it.'

Mike sighed. 'Well in the circumstances, I can hardly object, but I'll have something to say to that young lady later.'

***

They located Melanie, Christine and Stephanie in the hotel's chandeliered lounge. No-one else was present, so Paul explained the situation to the three of them. Then he looked at Melanie. 'What I'm asking you to do is strictly illegal, and we'll all understand if you refuse. If you do agree, I assure you we won't be revealing our methods to the police.'

Melanie's eyed sparkled in anticipation of the challenge. 'I'd love to have a go, especially if it helps to find the diamond. Let's all go to my room. I've just sent some material back to Wits by e-mail on my computer. The modem adapter is still connected to the telephone socket, so if you let me have Leo's number we can be up and running in a few seconds.'

Christine and Stephanie decided to remain in the lounge, so the three men escorted Melanie to her bedroom. Her computer was sitting alongside the hotel telephone on a table in the bedroom's small lounge area. Bryan handed her the copy of the Vandam order, and pointed to the e-mail code at the top of the page. Melanie switched on her computer and pressed a key on the telephone handset to get an open line. Then she activated the Internet e-mail facility on the Windows 99 program and keyed in the Vandam e-mail code.

They listened to the muted sounds of the digits as they were transmitted down the line. The computer's small dual-scan colour LCD screen went dark for a few seconds, and then displayed the Vandam Antiques logo and a menu containing two options, 'E-mail' and 'Bulletin Board'.

Using the computer's built-in tracker ball Melanie moved the screen arrow to the 'E-mail' option and pressed the enter key on her computer. The screen went dark again and then displayed the message 'TRANSMIT'.

Melanie fed a diskette into the computer. 'This is where you all look the other way,' she said. 'The disk contains my hacking protocol.' Melanie pressed the enter key and they heard the diskette drive run briefly. After a few seconds a Windows menu page giving access to Vandam Antiques office files and programs appeared on the screen. 'Bingo,' she murmured.

Melanie ignored the program options labelled 'E-mail', 'Wordpro', 'Stock List' and 'Client Directory', and selected the 'Accounts' one. She pressed the computer's 'enter' key. The screen went dark again and then displayed the message 'ENTER ACCESS CODE'.

'That's no surprise,' she said, and typed in 1, 2, 3, 4, 5 and pressed the enter key. The screen responded with the message 'ACCESS DENIED'.

'Just testing,' sighed Melanie. 'Now we'll have to think of a code word or phrase that a Russian ex-army colonel or an ex-KGB chief would use to protect his private data.'

'Why not a sequence of letters, or even numerals?' asked Jason.

'No, that's too easy to crack. It can be done in minutes with one of these gizmos.' She picked up a small electronic unit the size of a paperback book. 'You simply plug the device into the computer and instruct it to search through sequences of numbers. Depending on the number of numerals you chose, it will transmit millions of sequences in around five minutes flat until it hits the right one. If you tell it to do the same with letters, it will take longer as there are twenty-six in the alphabet compared with just ten numerals.'

'So code words are more secure,' agreed Bryan. 'We'd better all get a paper and pencil and get to work.'

Over the next two hours they came up with several dozen possible entry codes, including VESSOVSKI, LEOVANDAM, MOSCOW, MOSKVA, BARBAROSSA, SMERSH, RUSSALMAZ, LENINGRAD, ST PETERSBURG, DIAMANT, DIAMOND, GEMSTONE and combinations of these. None of them worked, however, and they decided to give the problem a rest and make another attempt the next morning.

* * *

When Jason returned to his room that night, he turned off the air conditioning unit. He was a light sleeper and sometimes found that the noise made by these units kept him awake. Jason undressed and had a shower. Then he picked up a book to read and climbed into bed. He lay for several minutes under the lightweight duvet with the book unopened on his lap as he tried to clear his mind of the code words that kept forcing their way into his consciousness. He was just about to switch off the light above the bedhead when there was a tap on his door. 'Come in — it's not locked,' he called out sleepily.

The door opened a few inches and Melanie slipped in. She shut the door behind her and turned the key. Jason's jaw dropped as he turned and saw the vision in pale green silk pyjamas standing in his room. 'I thought it was time we got to know each other better,' Melanie whispered, her cornflower blue eyes twinkling.

For once, Jason was completely at a loss for words. He threw off the thin duvet, dropped the book on the floor, and sat up on the edge of the bed. Melanie tiptoed across the room, her firm young breasts thrusting against the confines of her pyjama jacket as she moved towards him. The expression on Jason's face turned slowly from delighted surprise to embarrassment. He was wearing a pair of white boxer shorts which, while emphasizing the tan of his muscular body, did little to hide his reaction to Melanie's presence. Melanie saw the cause of his embarrassment and smiled. She reached across him and switched off the light. 'That's better - now move over and make room for me.'

Jason did as he was told, and in the faint starlight from the window, he lay back and watched with mounting interest while Melanie swiftly removed her pyjama top and trousers, and slipped naked into bed beside him. He could smell her perfume, and his head reeled under the combined onslaught to his senses.

Melanie was becoming concerned at his continuing silence. 'You're not upset I'm here?'

Jason cleared his throat. 'Of course not — I've been crazy about you ever since the Christmas visit. But do one thing for me, Melanie.'

She move closer to him until he could feel the cool pressure of her body against his. 'What's that?' she asked.

'Pinch me — I'm frightened that this may just be a dream, and I'll wake up soon.'

'I've a better idea. Why don't you kiss me. If this is a dream we might as well make some progress while it lasts.'

Jason sighed contentedly. He turned on his side, and traced the smooth soft contours of her face with his fingertips. Then in the half light he sought her lips with his and pulled her to him in their first intimate embrace. After a few seconds, Melanie pushed him gently away. Her hands searched for and found the button on his boxer shorts, and helped him struggle out of them.

'Fair's fair,' she said. I've got no nickers on.'

Jason levered himself up on one elbow. 'There are some condoms in my bedside drawer,' he announced, feeling bolder now.

'You are quite the boy scout,' giggled Melanie. 'I'm on the pill, but I do believe in safe sex. Just don't tell my mother.'

Jason smiled as he leaned across her. 'Parents sure are an embarrassment at times — my father actually offered me some condoms on my first date.' Then he kissed her breasts and moved his head down her body to nuzzle the warm soft triangle of fine hair at the junction of her thighs.

Melanie turned on her back and smiled up at him. 'So at last it's all systems go.'

By now Jason was becoming increasingly aware that he was close to losing control of a certain member of his body. He eased gently across Melanie's slender form and suddenly became conscious of her cool guiding hands. Jason shut his eyes in anticipation and entered her with an enthusiasm that made her moan with pleasure. Then, throwing caution to the winds, they began the wild roller-coaster ride of their young passion.

When they both finally got their breath back, Melanie looked up at Jason and kissed him tenderly. 'That was a bit energetic,' she murmured. 'Where did you learn your technique — in a ju-jitsu class?'

Jason smiled. 'Oh, I read a lot.'

Melanie wagged a finger at him. 'I'll give you five minutes to recover, my boy. Then we'll do it again, but this time more slowly — hey?'

Some time later, Jason lay listening to the sound of Melanie's regular breathing as she lay curled up at his side. His mind seemed unwilling to surrender to sleep, and he found himself going over the earlier events of the evening.

Suddenly he sat bolt upright. 'Of course — that's the answer,' he said out loud. 'Leo's interest in Russian composers.'

Melanie woke up with a start at the sound of his voice. 'What was that?'

'I've just remembered something Bryan said to me on the

flight over here. It was in Leo's police file. It seems he's a classical music buff. His favourite composer is Prokofiev.'

Melanie was now wide awake, and looked at him in surprise. 'You think that might be the access code. Could it be that simple?'

Jason was busy pulling on his boxer shorts. He threw Melanie's pyjamas to her. 'Come on — let's go to your room and try it out on the computer.'

Together they crept down the corridor and into Melanie's bedroom. Jason switched on the computer while Melanie opened the telephone line and keyed in the e-mail code. When the Vandam Antiques menu appeared on the screen, she selected 'E-mail', ran her hacking disk, and finally selected the accounts option again. The computer responded with the message 'ENTER ACCESS CODE'. She crossed her fingers and typed in 'PROKOFIEV'. The screen went dark for a moment and then displayed another menu labelled 'Accounts.'

'Bingo — we've cracked it!' whooped Jason.

Melanie studied the screen and read out the options. 'Orders, Invoices, Receipts, Tax Returns, Ledger.' She looked round at Jason. 'What do you think?'

'Print out the contents of the first and third sections — that should be enough.'

Melanie nodded and fed a sheaf of papers into the computer's built-in bubble-jet printer. 'You'd better get back to your room now, Jason. I'll start the printout, and we can pass it all over to Bryan at breakfast tomorrow.'

Jason bent over and kissed her. 'Agreed, but only on condition that we meet, same time same place, tomorrow night.'

'You've got a deal, my love,' smiled Melanie. She pressed a key and the computer began printing out the Vandam accounts.

CHAPTER 18

CAPE TOWN
Saturday 25 September, 1999

Melanie and Jason were first down to breakfast that morning. When their parents arrived, Melanie turned to Paul and waved some printed pages at him. 'Guess what Jason and I got up to last night after you all went to bed.'

Paul glanced at Mike and raised his eyebrows. 'I'm sure it wasn't scrabble.'

Jason turned slightly pink. 'We found the access code to Vandam's accounts. It was "Prokofiev", the name of Leo's favourite composer.'

At that moment, Bryan arrived. Paul took the sheets of paper from Melanie and handed them to him. 'Jason and Melanie have found the entry code for Vandam's accounts — the word we were looking for was "Prokofiev", and this is the printout.'

Bryan shook his head. 'I should have thought of that one — well done the two of you.' He sat down and started scanning the pages. 'There's got to be something here to incriminate Leo.'

After a few minutes he found what he was looking for, and triumphantly waved two of the pages in the air. 'Here's our hard evidence. The first page lists what appears to be shopping orders received from Leo's various clients. There are several under the name of Roman Perez in Brazil. One of them is dated July 20, 1980 and lists a 94-carat yellow diamond — that's got to be the stolen Golconda d'Or. Some of the other entries are for paintings — no doubt all stolen to order by our Russian friend and his team.'

Paul looked over his shoulder. 'There's another more recent diamond entry from Roman Perez dated September 5 1993. It lists a 530-carat colourless pear-shaped diamond. Unless I'm much mistaken, this must be the Cullinan I.'

'The dates match in nicely with the events,' agreed Bryan. 'The Golconda was stolen on October 18 1980, and the Tower Raid took place on February 6, 1994.'

Paul inspected the second page of the Vandam accounts. 'This is called "Receipts". It includes four very large payments from Roman Perez. One was made about a month on each side of the Golconda date, and the largest ones were made some three months before and a month after the Tower of London raid.'

Bryan carefully folded up the two pages and put them in his wallet. 'My guess is the "Receipts" page lists the advance and final payments for each of the two diamond transactions. Before I present this new material to our friend Inspector Duuren, I'm going to put through a call to the Yard. I want them to run a check on this Perez character.'

* * *

It was early afternoon before Bryan received a reply to his phone call to New Scotland Yard. When it came through, it was not from his own department. He was asked to wait, and then Sir Noel Lancaster, the Police Commissioner, came on the line.

'Sounds as if you have a line at last on the Phantom Diamond, DCI Raleigh.'

'Yes, sir, I have a feeling it's either here in Cape Town, or in Teresopolis, Brazil. Do you have anything for me on Senor Roman Perez?'

'We've been in touch with the Rio police. It seems that Perez senior was a very wealthy business man and a well-known art collector. He died of a heart attack back in August. There are two other items of news which I think you will agree point to South Africa. Our ex-KGB man, Vandam, attended the Perez funeral, and I'm told his son Juan has just flown out of Rio en route for Johannesburg.'

'That's all I need, sir. I'll get back to my SAP contact, Inspector Duuren — he's in the Diamond and Gold Branch of the Cape Town police. I'd appreciate it, however, if you could get someone to put pressure on the SAP. There appears to be a degree of reluctance to act against Vandam.'

'I'll get on to that immediately. The SAP commissioner is an old friend of mine. Incidentally, I've already passed on your information regarding the Perez-Vandam business to the Rio police. Young Juan Perez will be in for a nasty shock when he returns to Brazil.'

* * *

When Paul and Bryan re-visited Inspector Duuren later that afternoon, they found him in a more co-operative mood. Bryan showed him the two account pages detailing the diamond deals between Perez and Vandam, and then informed him of the results of the enquiries made to the Rio de Janeiro police.

Inspector Duuren carefully compared the dates on the Vandam accounts with the dates in his file of the diamond theft in Sydney and the raid on the Tower of London. He looked up at the two men. 'I won't embarrass you by asking how these details from Vandam's accounts were obtained. This extra evidence, and your proof that Vandam commissioned the CZ replica that was found in the royal sceptre, is enough for me to obtain a search warrant and arrange for a raid on his premises.'

A flicker of relief passed across Bryan's face. 'Can you tell me when you intend to mount the raid?'

'We will surprise Vandam and his associates at three o'clock tomorrow morning,' replied Inspector Duuren in his clipped Afrikaans accent. He smiled grimly at Bryan and Paul. 'In my country, we find our suspects more docile when wakened at this hour.'

Paul nodded. 'That sounds ideal. As my colleague here mentioned yesterday, I work for the Diamond Syndicate in London. We have a special interest in the recovery of the Phantom Diamond, which we suspect is in Vandam's possession. Because of the importance of its recovery to the UK Government, I must request that both DCI Raleigh and myself are present during the raid on Vandam's premises. I trust you have no objections to that?'

A look of annoyance passed briefly across the inspector's face. 'Your request is irregular, but I am instructed to co-operate fully with you, so my answer must be yes. Now please excuse me — there are many things to arrange if our visit to Vandam will be successful. Please be here just before three a.m. tomorrow.' He looked at Bryan's colourful outfit. 'I recommend you do not wear your best clothes for this excursion.'

* * *

At a quarter to three the next morning, Paul and Bryan left the Mount Nelson Hotel in their hire car and drove through the city's deserted streets to their rendezvous with Inspector Duuren. They were wearing dark blue coveralls borrowed from the hotel, and trainers. When they arrived at the police headquarters in Sea Point the inspector and his men were waiting for them. Paul wound down his window as the inspector walked up to their car. 'We are ready to leave now,' Duuren said, peering in at the two men. 'I have four armed men with me, and a driver.'

Paul gave him the thumbs up sign, and waited for Duuren and his team to climb into the small yellow police van and move off. He followed them as they drove through Sea Point's main thoroughfare of shops and restaurants and joined the narrow coast road. When they had left the street lights of neighbouring Bantry Bay behind them they found the night was much darker than they expected. Overhead, the moon, which had earlier provided some light was now hidden behind a thick cloud cover. On the right, Paul could just make out the white fluorescent crests of the Atlantic rollers as they broke on the rocky foreshore some thirty feet below the road.

They rounded the rocky promontory that separates Bantry Bay from Clifton, and a few minutes later were passing the darkened facades of the expensive villas built into the rock face of Cape Town's eastern seaboard. Paul saw the police van's rear lights flash on as it slowed and then stopped. He turned to Bryan. 'Looks as if we've arrived. I'll park well clear of the van in case there's trouble.' They got out and walked up the road to where Inspector Duuren was talking quietly to his men.

'I had a look at this property in daylight yesterday,' he said.

'The rock face up to the terrace is smooth and sheer, and there are no handholds. The lift cabin is stationed at the top, so there's no way we could use that even if it was operational. The only way up is to follow the lift track — the rails and the metal sleepers in between will give you hand and foot holds.' He looked round at his men. 'This is supposed to be a surprise visit, so no talking and no noise.'

Inspector Duuren turned to Paul and Bryan. 'I've left my driver in charge of the van in case anyone makes a break for it. The other four men and I will go up first. When we reach the lift cabin I'll give you a signal on my torch and start to deploy my squad around the house. Then you can join us for the break-in.'

Paul nodded in agreement. 'We've had Vandam in our sights for a long time. He's a slippery customer, and we appreciate being in at the kill — you may even find us useful as backup.'

Inspector Duuren sniffed and turned to the sergeant in charge of his team. 'Give me a boost up.' He placed his foot in the locked hands of the man and scrambled over the wall at the bottom of the lift track. One by one his men followed him and began the steep ascent to the house.

As they disappeared into the pitch black night, Bryan noticed that one of the men was carrying a stubby cast-iron battering ram in a sling over his back.

'The hell with waiting for Duuren to invite us up,' he whispered to Paul. 'I'm game to go now if you are.'

'You bet — if Duuren's going to make a frontal attack on the main entrance, I suggest we try moving left when we reach the lift cabin and head for the terrace.'

Halfway up the track, Paul and Bryan heard an exclamation ahead of them, followed by a muttered conversation. A few seconds later they joined the police team who had come to a halt.

'What's the problem,' whispered Bryan.

Inspector Duuren was clearly angry at their premature arrival. 'Bloody razor wire across the track,' he hissed.

Paul crawled out to the right-hand side of the track and using a small pen torch inspected the line of vertically positioned coils of barbed wire. The bases of the coils appeared to be tethered in circular pits placed between and on each side of the tracks.

'Looks as if the coils are released remotely from the top when the lift cabin is parked — just one more of Leo's little deterrents.' He groped in the pocket of his coveralls. 'Here, take these wire cutters — I thought they might come in useful.'

It took Duuren's men several minutes to clear a gap between the rails. Then they continued climbing the remaining forty feet to the top. When they finally reached the lift cabin, Paul waited for Bryan to reach him. The sky appeared lighter now, and they could just make out the contours of the rock face and the outline of the terrace rail above them.

Bryan moved up alongside Inspector Duuren. 'The surface of the rock is much rougher here. Paul and I will move out to the left and make for the terrace,' he whispered.

Duuren nodded. 'I could do with a diversion — but wait until I signal with my torch before you go in.'

Bryan moved back to Paul, and followed him onto the rock face. They had no difficulty in scrambling up the last few feet to the edge of the terrace. They peered cautiously over the top. The lounge and the upper windows were dark. Paul gave Bryan the thumbs up sign and climbed carefully over the terrace rail. He moved silently across the paving stones to the large picture window and beckoned Bryan to join him. They crouched together at the right-hand side of the window while Duuren and his team squeezed past the lift cabin and made for the front entrance.

A few seconds later, they saw a brief flash from Duuren's torch. Paul pulled a small jemmy from his pocket and inserted the blade between the handle of the sliding window and the frame. 'The window is bound to be alarmed,' he warned, and gave the jemmy a sharp blow with the heel of his fist.

The end of the door catch snapped off, and the window slid wide open. Almost simultaneously the lounge lights came on half-blinding the two men, and an alarm bell started ringing somewhere inside the house.

'Stay put,' hissed Paul. 'I'm going in.' He moved quickly into the lounge and looked around. There was only one door on the right. Paul half opened it and looked out into a short hallway. At the end of it he could dimly make out a flight of stairs leading to the upper floor. Above the sound of the alarm bell he suddenly became aware of the soft padding of bare feet as someone out of sight hurried down the stairs towards him. Paul retreated into the lounge and positioned himself behind the door.

The footsteps slowed and came to a halt. Then the muzzle of a forty-five calibre automatic pistol slowly appeared around the edge of the door. A passage in the SAS training manual flashed into Paul's mind. 'A gun at close quarters is always dangerous because of the unpredictable factors involved…'

Paul waited until the hand holding the gun came into view, then he slammed the door hard on it. There was an audible crack, and a cry of pain.

The gun fell to the floor and Paul kicked it across the room. He stepped back from the door just as it was flung wide open by Oleg Antonovitch. For a split second the two men faced each other. Oleg was wearing just a pair of black shorts.

'You again,' he snarled, his face distorted with pain and anger. 'This time, English, I finish you.'

He hurled himself at Paul, his weight carrying them both across the room. Paul lost his footing and they crashed onto a low wooden table. The weight of Oleg's body had momentarily winded him, and he lay helpless among the wreckage of the table as Oleg's hands went for his neck. Paul knew he had heard a bone break in Oleg's right hand when he slammed the door on him, and he was shocked by the man's seemingly undiminished brute strength as two thumbs pressed like steel clamps into his windpipe. He twisted sideways to get his knee between Oleg's legs and brought it up with all his remaining strength into the man's crutch.

Oleg screamed, his body doubled up in a reflex action, and his hands slackened their grip. Paul rolled clear and sucked in a lung-full of air. He heard the crash of splintering wood as Duuren's men broke down the entrance door. With his back to the window, Paul readied himself for another assault. Out of the corner of his eye he saw Bryan creep into the lounge and head for Oleg's gun. At that moment the alarm bell was turned off.

In his blind rage, Oleg was oblivious to everything now except the man crouched in front of him. He scrambled to his feet and picked up an ornamental dagger that was lying on top of a display cabinet.

'I too can fight dirty,' he growled, and crept towards Paul in a wrestler's stance with both arms spread wide, throwing the knife from hand to hand in a manoeuvre calculated to confuse his opponent. Without warning, Oleg launched himself at Paul like a missile, holding the knife in his uninjured left hand.

Paul's reactions had become adrenalin-sharp, and he fell prone to the floor and rolled to the right. Oleg was even faster, and managed to change direction in mid leap. His body crashed down on Paul, there was the sound of breaking glass, and then silence.

Paul extracted himself from under Oleg's body and got shakily to his feet. Oleg's head had smashed through the big lounge picture window and was bent upwards at an unnatural angle, the neck partly severed by the jagged edge of the glass. Paul looked down at the man lying dead at his feet. He could see the blood pulsing in a dark red stream from the jugular vein, and he felt exhausted and nauseous.

Bryan moved across the lounge to Paul's side and bent down over the body. 'Sorry I wasn't any help — it all seemed rather personal between the two of you.'

Paul massaged his bruised neck. 'Yes — he's the Russian heavy who nearly killed me in Peking several years ago — but that's another story.'

Inspector Duuren walked into the lounge followed by one of his men pushing a handcuffed Clive Drake. He stopped in surprise when he saw Oleg's twisted body. 'I see you take no prisoners, Mr Remington. That must be the third member of the Vandam team.' He looked sternly his sergeant. 'Get a sheet or something over that body. Then get an ambulance here as quickly as possible.'

Bryan turned to him. 'Where is Leo Vandam?'

'Nowhere to be found — we've searched the place.'

'And the diamond?'

'Not a trace so far — we will make a more detailed search tomorrow as soon as it gets light.'

Just then they heard the clang of an opening garage door

followed by the roar of a racing engine. Paul ran out of the lounge and hung over the balcony rail. He was just in time to see a black Mercedes sports car appear on the road below, its headlamps scything through the dark night. The car swung left and raced down the coast road in the direction of Camps Bay. Bryan and Inspector Duuren joined him on the terrace.

'How on earth did he get down to the garage without anyone seeing him?' exclaimed Bryan.

Paul grabbed Bryan's arm. 'I'll show you.' He led them through the lounge into the hallway. 'Where is the kitchen?' he asked Inspector Duuren.

The inspector pointed to one of the doors leading off the hallway to the left. They all followed Paul through into the roomy kitchen. He walked across to a fitted cupboard under the kitchen window and pulled open the unit's hopper door. 'Leo Vandam went down the garbage chute — it exits at the side of the garage.'

Paul pulled out a length of knotted nylon rope, one end of which was tied to a steel 'U' bolt set in the concrete floor. 'This was Leo's emergency escape route,' explained Paul, turning to Inspector Duuren. 'I suggest you contact your people and alert all the airports and shipping terminals.'

Inspector Duuren sighed. 'I will do that immediately, of course. I will also have an all points alert put out for the car. If the driver of our van failed to get the registration number of the Mercedes, we can get it from our records, although I expect Vandam's got another car hidden away somewhere close by.'

'Yesterday we heard that Juan Perez had flown out of Rio for Jo'burg,' commented Bryan. 'It's my guess he's heading for a rendezvous with Vandam. At this point in the game, I'd rather neither of them were arrested unless they attempt to leave the country. While they're still at liberty, one or the other should lead us to the Phantom Diamond.'

When they returned to the lounge, Paul pointed to the mute handcuffed figure of Clive Drake who was slumped in one of the chairs. 'What about him?'

'He told me he's prepared to talk in exchange for a more lenient sentence when he comes to trial,' answered Inspector

Duuren. 'He's already confirmed that Vandam had an appointment to meet Juan Perez some time next week. He also gave me the combination of the safe here — I've checked, but it's empty. All the computer records have been wiped clean as well.'

Bryan shook his head in annoyance, and spoke directly to Clive Drake. 'You're not in a very good position to make a bargain. It's quite possible you'll be extradited to the UK where you will stand trial for the murder of at least eight people. My advice is for you to co-operate fully, and pray that you only face charges in South Africa.'

Clive Drake raised his manacled hands and adjusted his glasses. He tore his gaze away from the body of his Russian colleague and looked up with a nervous smile at Bryan. 'Tell me what you want to know.'

'Where is the big colourless diamond?'

Clive took a deep breath. 'Until a few days ago it was in Leo's safe. I think he has taken it with him to give back to Juan Perez. Juan wanted it cut into several smaller stones and sold, but Leo had difficulty in finding a diamond cutter willing to do the job.'

'When and where is Leo meeting Juan Perez,' asked Paul.

'That I don't know,' answered Clive. 'I think he intended phoning him today to fix the rendezvous.'

Inspector Duuren interrupted. 'I'll contact Jo'burg's domestic terminal. If Juan books out from there on a scheduled flight to rendezvous with Vandam, we will have them both.'

'I just hope it will be that simple,' commented Paul, 'but I've an uneasy feeling that Juan and Leo may have a few more tricks up their sleeves.'

'One more thing,' said Duuren. 'It is a formality, of course, but I will need your and Mr Raleigh's statements for my report on this affair. I would request you both visit our Sea Point headquarters in the morning.'

CHAPTER 19

CAPE — EASTERN TRANSVAAL
Sunday 26 September, 1999

Dressed in only a T-shirt and shorts, and with his feet bare, Leo Vandam sat grim-faced behind the wheel of his black Mercedes as he threw the car around the bends of the twisting coast road. Keeping one hand on the wheel, he attempted to brush off the evidence of his descent down the rubbish chute. Despite his rule that all wet garbage should be bagged before being put down the chute, he had emerged from the refuse room next to the garage festooned with reminders of meals past. The temporary surge of elation he had felt at his escape had rapidly been replaced by a feeling of anger.

Despite his own good relations with the local police inspector, and Clive Drake's connections with the Diamond and Gold Branch of the SAP, he had received no warning of the raid. This had thrown his well laid plans into disarray, and had now forced him to put one of his contingency plans into action.

At this hour of the morning there was hardly any on-coming traffic, and the few cars he met signalled their presence well in advance with their headlamp beams. He flung his car into another double-bend, automatically adjusting its line as he sliced across the corners from apex to apex. At least, he brooded, he had left no evidence behind at the Eagles Nest that could be used to detain his two associates for more than a few hours. If there was any trouble, his attorney had access to funds in the business account should he need to arrange bail for Clive and Oleg.

His most pressing problem right now was to avoid any road blocks that might have been set up by the police. Once he was clear of the immediate area his next priority was to meet Juan Perez at their selected rendezvous in just under three days time.

His original plan had been to fly from Cape Town International Airport to Durban on Tuesday morning and then take a leisurely drive in a hire car to the rendezvous. He silently congratulated himself for not revealing the details of this meeting to his partners in crime, so neither of them could now be forced to reveal his movements. The prompt delivery of the five yellow diamonds to Juan Perez was essential if he was to defuse Juan's threat of denouncing him to Interpol. But even this threat had already lost some of its impact in view of his own contingency plans to leave the country. In any case his possession of the stones was just one more complication in the course of action he was now being forced to follow, and he would certainly be able to breathe a lot easier once he had rid himself of the remaining evidence of the stolen Golconda d'Or.

Leo felt in the breast pocket of his T-shirt for the package that concealed the second piece of evidence he was now forced to put into temporary hiding before his meeting with Juan. If he was stopped with this in his possession, he would lose one of his trump cards. An audacious idea suddenly struck him — he would conceal his premier bargaining piece in a place so public that no-one would ever think of searching there.

The sky had begun to lighten in the east when Leo reached Hout Bay. He made a left turn off the main road, extinguished his lights, and drove into a newly built residential estate. He stopped at one of the detached bungalows and swung the car into the brick-paved driveway of a double garage. Using a remote control unit, Leo opened the door and drove the Mercedes into the garage alongside a metallic silver-grey Toyota Corolla. He had chosen the Corolla as back-up car because of its ubiquitous presence on the South African roads.

Leo opened the Toyota's boot and pulled out a holdall containing an overnight bag, a change of clothes and a small briefcase. He slipped the package from his breast pocket into the briefcase, and then changed into a long-sleeved white shirt, a pair of brown slacks, and a fawn colour jacket. Next, he hastily pulled on a pair of socks and shoes, thankful that he had taken the precaution to include these last items in his emergency kit. Finally, he checked the contents of the briefcase. Satisfied that the forged passport and the emergency pack of banknotes in a range of hard currencies were still there, he bundled his discarded clothes into the holdall and locked it in the boot of the Mercedes. He patted the bonnet of the sleek sports car lovingly. 'Au revoir for the time being,' he murmured and climbed stiffly into the Toyota. He gunned the engine, backed out of the garage, and closed the double door with the control unit.

Dawn had begun to break as he continued his journey southwards skirting the broad waters of Hout Bay and climbing through the mountains to Chapman's Peak. From there he cut across the long finger of land that ends at Cape Point, and headed east until he picked up the N2 motorway. Leo followed the road as it wound its way up the steep incline to the Sir Lowry Pass. At the top, he drove into a layby and pulled a map out of the glove compartment. He climbed out of the car and stretched his legs in the early morning sunshine. With the map spread across the car's bonnet Leo decided his best plan was to continue heading east along South Africa's southern seaboard. Any roadblocks, he reasoned, would have been set up assuming he was heading either for Cape Town's International Airport, or along the N9 to Johannesburg.

By mid afternoon he arrived in the old colonial town of George, and had put two-hundred and fifty miles between himself and the Eagles Nest. Leo checked his map again, and then headed north through the ostrich farms of Oudtshourn. That evening, as the light was beginning to fade, he booked himself into a motel in the outskirts of Beaufort West. He had an evening meal in the motel's adjoining restaurant and then retired exhausted to bed.

Next morning Leo was up early. He breakfasted and then listened to the seven o'clock news on the radio. There was nothing about the raid on his headquarters in Clifton, but that did not surprise him. There were plenty of more important and newsworthy events happening in the awakening giant of the new rainbow republic. Leo was pleased he had covered a third of his intended journey without the need to take more than common-sense evasive action. He had carefully kept his speed well within the limits so as to avoid any unwelcome attention from the traffic police. Now he had one more important task to accomplish before he met Juan Perez in the Eastern Transvaal on the following day.

Leo got back in his car and headed north again. Fifty miles out of Beaufort West he forked left onto the N13, and continued in a northerly direction, making a short diversion off the main road at midday to have lunch in a restaurant at the side of the Smartt Syndicate Reservoir.

The sun was beginning to set again as he entered the outskirts of Kimberley. He drove into the centre of the town and booked himself into the historic old Kimberley Club which Cecil Rhodes and Barney Barnato patronised back in the town's diamond pioneering days of the 1880s. Leo had stayed in the Kimberley Club once before when he first arrived in South Africa, and was aware that its security arrangements were less formal than those of the more modern hotels in the town, a fact which would fit in with his plans for that night.

He had a meal in the Club's dinning room, and a nightcap in the famous old bar before retiring to his chintz and Victoriana bedroom. At two o'clock the next morning he was awakened by his wristwatch alarm. The town of Kimberley lies at an altitude of four-thousand feet, and even in the height of summer, the nights can be chilly. Leo dressed and pulled on his jacket. He checked the bulge in his pocket, and moving silently, he let himself out of the Club and walked to where he had parked his car several hundred yards away. He started the engine, and drove slowly off into the night. When he returned an hour later, his coat pocket bulged no more.

* * *

The following day Leo was on the road by five in the morning driving north out of Kimberley on the N13. Sixty miles southwest of Johannesburg he took to the smaller roads and navigating with the map made a wide westerly detour to meet the Pretoria to Maputo highway at Witbank. By four o'clock Leo's mood lightened considerably as he drove through the entrance to the government-run holiday resort Overvaal Blydepoort in the Eastern Transvaal. The resort was sited in the Blyde River Canyon nature reserve, and consisted of stone chalets built along the side of the canyon. Within the complex was a restaurant, a small supermarket for self-caterers, a swimming pool, riding stables, and a 9-hole golf course. However, the reason Leo chose Overvaal for his meeting with Juan Perez was the small grass landing strip, complete with windsock, on the plateau above the resort.

When Juan flew in on a chartered four-seater Cessna later that afternoon, Leo was standing at the windward end of the landing strip to greet him. The high-wing plane did a low pass overhead to check out the treacherous wind currents that gusted out of the canyon, and then came in low and bounced a few times as the wheels of its tri-carriage made contact with the uneven surface. The plane taxied to a halt, and Juan Perez climbed out followed by the pilot.

Leo shook hands with Juan and they waited while the pilot hammered two metal pegs in the ground and attached a nylon rope from them to a hook on each of the plane's wingtips. 'The winds on the escarpment are rather unpredictable,' he explained. Juan and the pilot followed Leo to his car at the end of the field and they drove down past the riding stables and stopped at the restaurant.

The pilot got out of the car and squinted up at the fast moving clouds. 'If it's OK with you, I'd like to get moving again before too long. The weather is beginning to close in.'

'I'll be back for you in an hour,' promised Leo. He and Juan drove on to the chalet he had rented for the next few nights. Leo parked the car in the shade at the side of the chalet, and led Juan into the open-plan lounge. He took two tins of beer from the refrigerator in the small kitchen, found a couple of glasses in a fitted cupboard above the stove, and placed them on a table between the two easy chairs in the lounge. 'Please to be seated.' He waved to the chairs, and sat down facing the handsome young man. 'How are things with you?'

Juan pulled a face. 'Not brilliant — the lawyers are still haggling over my father's will. It seems there's no way I can break it and get my hands on the capital.'

Leo sighed. 'I'm sorry to hear that, Juan. I too have my

problems.' Juan looked concerned. 'You have brought me the money?'

'That was certainly my intention, but three days ago my headquarters were raided by the police. I was lucky to get out, and as far as I know my two colleagues are now under arrest.'

Juan slammed his tin of beer down on the table in anger. 'But when we talked on the phone last week you said you had the deal all set with a buyer.'

'Calm yourself — the deal is still on, but there's no way I can make the contact myself now.'

Leo pulled a cloth jewellery roll from his pocket and unwrapped it. 'Here are your five yellow diamonds — it's up to you now to make the delivery and collect your money.' He handed Juan the stones and a business card. 'This is the dealer's name and address — he's in Pretoria. Tell him I couldn't make it — he knows the stones are yours.'

Juan's anger slowly subsided. He took the diamonds and the card from Leo, and put them in the money belt he wore round his waist. 'What about the big diamond,' he asked.

'That is safe for the moment in a place where no-one will find it. But I have to tell you that the chances of hiring a cutter who will do what you want are very thin. I suggest you let me find another collector, like your late father, and then there will be no need to have it re-cut.'

Juan sniffed. 'It seems I've got no choice but to trust you. What are your immediate plans?'

Leo shrugged his broad shoulders. 'I'll stay here for a few days until things have quietened down. There are some interesting tourist places I would like to visit in the area — God's window, Bourke's potholes and the old gold mining town of Pilgrims Rest. After that, I'll back-track to Kimberley, collect the big diamond from its hiding place, and slip out of the country through the back door into Mozambique. It's unlikely that anyone will be watching the port of Maputo. Then I'll set up a new base — probably in Argentina.'

'Just let me know where I can get hold of you,' said Juan, grimly. 'We still have some unfinished business between us — and please don't force me to call on the services of the police to find you.'

Leo ignored the threat, knowing there was little Juan could do to him once he was out of South Africa. He drove him back to the restaurant and picked up the pilot. When they arrived at the airstrip, the pilot unhooked the wing tethers and stowed the rope and pegs in the plane. Juan shook hands with Leo while the pilot warmed up the plane's engine and ran through the pre-flight checks.

'Take good care of the big diamond,' said Juan, and climbed into the plane. Leo watched as the Cessna taxied to the far end of the grass airstrip. He saw it turn into the wind and heard the engine roar under full throttle. The pilot released the brakes, and the plane rolled forward and began to pick up speed. Leo raised his hand in salute as the machine lifted off and flew past him.

He turned and watched the Cessna disappear over the rim of the escarpment. 'I have a strong presentiment Juan and I have had our last meeting,' he muttered to himself.

CHAPTER 20

CAPE TOWN
Wednesday 29 September, 1999

It was mid-morning, and Paul and Bryan were sitting in Inspector Duuren's office in Sea Point discussing the previous weeks events. 'Did you get anything from Clive Drake on Vandam's movements?' asked Bryan.

The inspector shook his head. 'Drake professes to know nothing.' He paused for a moment in contemplation. 'In the old South Africa, I would have the truth out of him by now.'

Paul glanced at Bryan. 'I thought those methods were reserved for non-whites,' he said.

Duuren laughed. 'When it came to serious interrogation, we were more even-handed.'

'What about the Phantom Diamond — do you think he still has it?'

The inspector raised both his hands in resignation. 'Your guess is as good as mine. The safe was empty as you know, and he managed to wipe everything off his computer's hard disk before he left. Presumably any back-up disks that existed were in the briefcase he took with him. It almost looks as if he was preparing to disappear, even before our raid.'

'And what of Juan Perez?' asked Bryan.

'There I do have some news,' replied Duuren. 'He flew back to Johannesburg yesterday in a private plane. We intercepted both Perez and the pilot. The pilot said his plane was chartered by a Mr Juan Prospero to fly him to the Overvaal holiday resort in the Eastern Transvaal. The flight plan he filed confirmed this. We immediately phoned the resort, but they had no record of a Prospero, a Perez or a Vandam staying there, so presumably Vandam used a false name also.'

'They were, however, aware of a light plane using their airstrip, and said it had been arranged in advance by the pilot.'

'Did you have Perez searched?'

'Yes. I had warned security at the airport to be on the alert as you suggested last Sunday. The police found five yellow diamonds on him, but nothing else of consequence, except the business card of a diamond dealer in Pretoria. Juan Perez said he was trying to find a buyer for the stones. When he was asked why he used a false name, he claimed he was trying to keep his movements confidential as he was carrying high-value goods. After holding him overnight, the Jo'burg airport police decided they did not have sufficient grounds to detain him further, and he was released that morning.'

Bryan turned to Paul. 'The yellow diamonds must have come from the Golconda d'Or. Isn't there any way of proving that?'

Paul shook his head. 'There are many so-called fingerprint methods of identifying a polished diamond, but they all depend on the pre-existence of a scientific analysis or record of the diamond under suspicion. In one method, developed by Roy Edelstone of the Hatton Garden Diamond Certification Company, one of the diamond's facets, usually the largest one, is photographed under a specially adapted microscope using what is called Nomarski interference contrast illumination. This makes minute surface defects in the stone's crystal structure clearly visible. These defects usually penetrate deep into the diamond, so even if it's recut, they're still visible. The fingerprint photograph can then be compared with one taken on a suspect stone and used to prove that it is either the same stone, or was recut from it.'

'So there's no chance of linking the five yellow diamonds found on Juan Perez with the Golconda?' asked Bryan

'Only by the circumstantial evidence we've accumulated so far, and that would most probably not be sufficient in a court of law,' answered Paul. 'In any case, our brief is to recover the big stone we call the Phantom Diamond. The way it keeps eluding us makes me realise the name was well chosen.'

Inspector Duuren picked up a fax sheet from his desk. 'This may interest you. It was sent to us by the Kimberley police this morning. It seems there was a mysterious break-in at their Open Mine Museum two days ago. Someone managed to bypass the alarm systems in the Diamond Pavilion and open the main display cabinet.'

'What was taken?' asked Bryan.

'That's the mystery. The curator and his staff have carefully checked the exhibits against the inventory, and everything has been accounted for.'

There was something in this report that struck Paul as vaguely familiar, but he was unable to pin it down. 'Well, inspector, we'll just have to hope that Leo Vandam breaks cover soon. In the meanwhile, DCI Bryan Raleigh and I will use the time to see a little more of your lovely country. We'll let you know where we are over the next few days, and you can keep us up to date with any developments.'

Inspector Duuren nodded in agreement. He pointed to the paperwork that had piled up on his desk. 'I also have ways of filling my time until Vandam re-appears.'

* * *

Paul and Bryan had arranged to meet the others for lunch in the hotel's Oasis Restaurant by the pool. When they were all seated at a table on the terrace, Stephanie turned to Paul. 'So what's the news — have you got any closer to finding the Phantom Diamond?'

'In one word, no,' replied Paul. 'All the exits from the country are being watched for Vandam, but until he shows himself, there's little that Bryan and I can do at the moment.' Paul frowned 'Inspector Duuren told us there'd been a mysterious break-in at Kimberley's Diamond Pavilion in the Open Mine Museum.'

He pulled a tourist map from his pocket and studied it. 'When Leo left the Eagles Nest in a hurry last Sunday morning, we now know he was heading for the Eastern Transvaal to meet Juan Perez.' Paul moved his finger across the map from Cape Town to the Blyde River Canyon. 'It wouldn't have been much of a detour for him to have visited Kimberley en route.'

'But why should he have done that?' asked Christine.

'I don't know, but if he did, it would confirm this strange déjà vu feeling I have that there's something familiar about the Kimberly break-in.'

Paul smiled. 'Perhaps I'm just looking for a good excuse for us to visit Kimberley on the expense account — I've always wanted to see the Big Hole.'

'What a good idea,' agreed Melanie. 'We've been there a couple of times, so we can act as your guides.'

Mike looked at his watch. 'There's a flight leaves here every afternoon for Kimberley via Port Elizabeth. Why don't we all pack a few overnight things and catch it. We can leave the rest of our luggage with the hotel reception.'

Christine got up from the table. 'I'll make a call and book us into the New Kimberley Hotel. While I'm doing that, you and Paul can make the flight reservations.'

Jason nudged Melanie. 'Let's hope our rooms are not too far apart — I like to conserve my energy.'

* * *

Paul had been making a daily phone call to Steven Heming in London to check there were no problems with his work load. After Mike had made sure there were seven seats booked for them on the Kimberley flight, Paul rang Steven to say he would be away from Cape Town for a few days.

'How are things with you Steve,' he asked when he heard the familiar voice on the phone.

'No problems — except for yesterday when Sir James went berserk among the female sorters and had to be locked in the vault.'

Paul chuckled. 'Glad to hear everything's normal. I'm off to Kimberley for a day or two, so just keep at it — and spare a thought for all of us here suffering under blue skies and a hot sun. By the way, how's the weather with you?' The instrument crackled with Steven's reply, and Paul put the receiver down quickly.

CHAPTER 21

KIMBERLEY
Wednesday 29 September, 1999

In 1871, when the South African diamond rush was in full spate, over five thousand diggers were recovering diamonds along the banks of the Vaal, Modder and Orange rivers. In the same year, a further massive source of diamonds was found in and around a farm in the north-west corner of Cape Province. Unlike previous diamond finds, this one was not associated with a river, and became known as the first 'dry' digging. Over the next two years an encampment of tents and a primitive town had sprung up around the site of the farm, and in 1873 the town was formally named Kimberley after the British Secretary for the Colonies, the Earl of Kimberley. There were hundreds of claims staked on the site, and the top of what turned out to be a massive diamond pipe was being mined deeper and deeper. With the multitude of individual claims there was always the danger of adjacent diggings collapsing and burying miners.

As miners made their fortunes and retired from the scene, their claims were bought up and amalgamated into mining consortiums, and safer techniques were introduced. After much wheeling and dealing between characters such as Cecil Rhodes, Barney Barnato and Alfred Beit, these companies were eventually combined under Rhodes' control into one large concern. The resulting massive mine, as it went deeper, eventually became known as the Big Hole of Kimberley. After forty years of intensive production, which yielded nearly three tons of diamonds, the Kimberley mine was finally closed in 1914, its mining shaft having reached a depth of just over three-thousand, six-hundred feet.

When Mike and his party arrived at Kimberley's small airport late on Wednesday afternoon they picked up two hire cars and drove the three miles into town to their hotel. The New Kimberley Hotel was one of the first modern ones to be built in the town in the mid 1970s. Its interior design for those days was unusual, the cavernous interior reaching up some eighty feet to a glass dome, and all the bedrooms leading off interior balconies which looked down on the restaurants and lounge below.

After Mike and his party had booked into their rooms, they all met up again for an evening meal in the hotel's 'Five Mines' restaurant. While they were waiting to be served, Mike produced a map of Kimberley and pointed out some of the town's attractions. 'The place is full of history,' he said. 'A lot of the original buildings are still standing, and there are three lovely old museums. Among the monuments there's a bronze statue of miners holding up a massive rock sieve that's worth seeing, and on the eastern edge of the town there's the famous Big Hole where it all began.'

'That's the site of the Open Mine Museum,' said Christine. 'It's the main reason why Kimberley attracts so many visitors each year.'

'It's also the main reason why we're here,' Bryan reminded them. 'Paul and I are supposed to be checking out the break-in at the Museum's Diamond Pavilion.'

Melanie winked at Jason and yawned. 'It's been a long day, folks, so if you'll excuse me I'm off to bed with a good book.'

* * *

Later that night, Jason tapped gently on Melanie's door.

'If you're handsome, come in,' Melanie called out. 'The door's unlocked.'

'You really should be more security conscious,' chided Jason, entering the room. Melanie was stretched out on her bed reading a book. The night was hot and she was wearing one of her more skimpy see-through nighties.

Jason moved across the room and sat on the bed beside her. Melanie raised her head to receive his kiss. 'Now stop lecturing me,' she pouted. 'I have enough of that from my parents.' She laid her book down and looked critically at his karate-style pyjama jacket and baggy shorts. 'If you want our relationship to survive, you'll have to let me re-organise your wardrobe, Jason.'

Jason sighed and took her hand. 'That's just it — do we have a future together, Melanie?' He leaned forward and kissed her firm young breasts through the thin cotton material of her nightdress. 'We have to be practical — you are here in South Africa, and I'll soon be returning to the UK.'

Melanie's expression softened. She reached out her hand and brushed back the auburn hair that had fallen across his forehead. 'I think we have got a future together, Jason. But before I tell you why, let me ask you a direct question. We've had a great time together these last few days, and I don't just mean in bed. But are you in love with me?'

'Of course I am, Melanie. I think I always have been, even when I was a young boy and you called me an irritating brat.'

'I can take that as a definite yes, then?' teased Melanie. 'Now it's your turn to ask me.'

Jason turned slightly pink. 'I know I'm four years younger than you, Melanie, but do you feel the same way about me?'

'Of course I do, you idiot, or you wouldn't be sitting on my bed right now.'

'There's something else I want you to know, Melanie. When I'm qualified and I've got a decent job, I'm going to hop on a plane to South Africa and ask you to marry me.'

'You won't need to hop on a plane, my love. When father retires next year, we're going to return to the UK for good. That's why he didn't sell Aunt Muriel's London flat when she left it to him in her will. We're going to make it our UK home — we'll be practically neighbours this time next year!'

Melanie laughed at Jason's expression of delight. 'Now take off your jacket — I want to check you didn't get burnt when you stripped off yesterday at the Waterfront.'

Jason obeyed her and she looked him over critically. 'You're beginning to get a decent colour at last.'

'Would you like to check out the white bits now,' he asked.

'I'll get round to that in a moment,' Melanie countered. She extinguished the light and slipped off her nightdress.

* * *

Next morning they all met up in the hotel's foyer restaurant. When they had finished breakfast, Mike cleared away the plates to make room for his map of Kimberley.

'As Bryan pointed out yesterday, the official reason we're here in Kimberley is to check out the break-in at the Diamond Pavilion, but there's no reason why we shouldn't visit one or two other places on the way to the Open Mine Museum.'

Paul nodded in agreement. 'What do you have in mind?'

Mike pointed to the Market Square on the map. 'Let's leave the cars behind and take a walk from here to Market Square — that will give you some idea of the town. We can go via the Civic Centre and visit the diamond sorting offices in Kimberley House. That's the tall monolith of a building you saw from the plane just before we landed yesterday. I know the chief valuator — if he's in, I'll ask if he can show us around.'

'Their collection of unusual diamonds is worth seeing, and so is their automatic weighing department,' added Melanie.

'After that,' continued Mike, 'we can catch a tram in Market Square. That will give you another view of the town, and take us right into the Open Mine Museum.'

When they arrived in the cool reception hall of Kimberley House, Mike asked the security officer on duty to check if his friend John Galsworthy was available. 'Tell him, it's Mike Reece from the Pretoria Mining Company,' he said.

While they were waiting, Christine pointed to the large mural over the entrance. 'That's an abstract painting representing all the aspects of diamond mining — the cluster of small triangles depicts the trigon markings you can see on the surfaces of uncut diamonds.'

A few minutes later a stocky fair-haired man appeared at the reception desk. When he caught sight of Mike his round cherubic face broke into a broad smile. 'Good God,' he exclaimed, his blue eyes twinkling with mischief. 'I thought they'd buried you long ago in that mine of yours.' He walked round the reception desk and embraced his old friend.

'This is Detective Chief Inspector Bryan Raleigh,' said Mike, making the introductions. 'You know my wife Christine and daughter Melanie, of course. This is Paul Remington and his wife Stephanie from the Diamond Syndicate's headquarters in London, and this is their son Jason.'

When they had all shaken hands, John Galsworthy took them up to his office on the fourth floor and organised coffee for them all. 'So is this your first time in Kimberley?' he asked Paul.

'Yes, but it's a bit of a busman's holiday, really,' explained Paul. 'Bryan and I are in South Africa on the trail of a large stolen diamond. When we heard of the break-in at the Open Mine Museum it seemed a good excuse to visit the town.'

'That break-in was certainly a strange business. Whoever did it was an expert at disabling alarm systems. There were some high-value diamonds in the pavilion, including the big uncut 616 carat stone, and of course the famous 10.73 carat Eureka — the first diamond to be discovered in South Africa — but nothing was taken.'

John Galsworthy picked up his phone and dialled a number. He glanced at Paul. 'I'll get someone to lay out our collection of special diamonds. After you've seen those you can take a look at our automatic weighing department — it's similar to the Syndicate's one in London, but we made a few modifications.'

The special diamonds in the Kimberley House collection had been culled from the vast volume of rough diamonds that had passed through the company's sorting departments over the years. They included a full spectral range of coloured stones together with examples of the strange distorted shapes in which some diamonds form deep in the earth. Christine was particularly impressed by a large pale blue stone with a hole through the centre. 'That would make a great pendant,' she said, picking up the diamond. 'But not on my salary,' whispered Paul. 'Just put it down before we get arrested.'

When they got to the automatic weighing room, Jason showed more interest. He had just started robotics and artificial intelligence in his electronic engineering course, and was intrigued to see the thirty computer-controlled machines at work, each one extracting diamonds one at a time from a feed hopper, placing them on an electronic balance, and then dropping them into the appropriate division of a plastic output tray.

'They're using a vacuum pick-and-place system to handle the diamonds,' he commented to his father.

'Yes, it's an interesting variation on the vibratory feeder method the Syndicate uses in its London weighers,' replied Paul.

Bryan turned to John Galsworthy. 'I know a little from Paul about the London operation, but what happens to all your diamonds here once they've been weighed,' he asked.

'Some of them are offered at the Sights held here in Kimberley at five-weekly intervals,' explained John. 'The rest are sent to the Syndicate's offices in London, where they're mixed in with similar diamonds of the same colour, shape, quality and weight from other sources around the world.'

* * *

When they left Kimberley House, Mike led them through the centre of the town to Market Square. There they caught an orange-painted tram which trundled them at a leisurely pace past some of the old houses at the edge of the town until it arrived at the entrance to the Open Mine Museum. Over the years the museum had slowly evolved from a small collection of restored shacks and shops which in the late 1880s provided the town of Kimberly with the necessities of life. The buildings were now arranged in a realistic re-creation of the streets that had once formed the nucleus of the small mining town of Kimberley.

Mike ushered his group into the museum's entrance kiosk. He purchased the admission tickets and waited while they all signed the visitor's book.

Leo Vandam entered the kiosk just as Mike and his party were leaving. He had arrived in Kimberley that morning after lying low for several days at the Overvaal holiday resort. Although it was his intention to retrieve the Cullinan diamond from its hiding place that night, a strange premonition had drawn him to the museum. He glanced curiously at the group of people who were just leaving the kiosk. As they filed out of the door, one of them turned to speak to his companion. Leo sucked in his breath sharply as he suddenly recognised the man.

He walked over to the visitors' book and ran his finger down the last few entries. 'Paul Remington,' he hissed. 'The man from the Diamond Syndicate's Special Operations department.' Leo hurriedly purchased a ticket from the counter, and, keeping a safe distance between himself and Paul's group, he followed them as they wandered through the museum's open-air recreation of old Kimberley.

The group of streets contained a hotel and a variety of stores, including a chemist's shop with rows of neatly labelled glass and porcelain jars holding the chemicals and potions which were the basic treatment for ailments in those far off days. There was a diamond buyer's corrugated iron hut, complete with its portable twin-pan diamond scales, receipt books and a framed diamond buyer's licence. Next to this was the 'Diggers Retreat' with bar, dummy barman and taped raucous music. Round the next corner they discovered a jail house, a small chapel, a pawnbroker's shop and a haberdasher's.

Melanie stopped in front of the haberdasher's shop window, and pointed. 'Just look at those outsize bloomers,' she exclaimed.

'Passion killers — an early form of Victorian birth control,' commented Paul, drily.

Mike looked at his watch. 'I think it's time we had a look at the Big Hole. They say it's one of the few man-made features visible from space.'

The visitors' platform, surrounded by a wire safety cage, gave them a view down the friable shale walls of the old mine to the surface of the flood water some five-hundred feet below. Visible just beyond the western edge of the hole's one mile perimeter, the houses and buildings of Kimberley appeared to be on the point of collapsing into the gaping hole in front of them.

Jason walked past the large board listing the mine's vital statistics and took several photographs of the hole through the wire safety fence at the end of the platform.

Melanie shook her head when he beckoned her to join him. 'I'm not happy looking down from a great height,' she confessed.

'That's OK,' said Jason. 'I'm not happy with moths.' He

sauntered back and took a group photograph of everyone standing in front of the display board.

Bryan looked at his museum guide. 'The Diamond Pavilion is just the other side of the transport and mining hall building. Shall we justify our presence here by having a look at it?'

Mike, Paul and Jason agreed to the suggestion, but the women decided to take another look at the streets of Victorian shops. 'We'll meet you in the coffee shop by the kiosk in half an hour,' said Christine.

The main display unit in the Diamond Pavilion was a large circular glass cabinet containing samples of uncut and polished diamonds. Included in the collection was a display of fancy-colour diamonds, and several items of jewellery. Among the rough stones was the 616-carat Kimberley Octahedron, labelled as the world's largest uncut diamond. In the polished section, pride of place was given to the 10.73-carat brilliant-cut Eureka diamond, which put South Africa on the map in 1867 as a source of diamonds. Other less costly exhibits in the cabinet were glass models of famous diamonds mined in South Africa.

There were several other visitors in the pavilion when the four men arrived. A middle-aged woman was busy identifying the larger of the glass diamond replicas to her young daughter.

'That's the big Cullinan which was found in the Premier Mine,' she said. 'And those are the nine principle stones that were cut from it.'

'Are they real diamonds?' asked the young girl.

'No, dear. They're just glass models, but they certainly look like the real thing — especially the big one. That's the diamond mounted in the British royal sceptre.'

Paul was standing just behind the woman and her daughter. When she moved away he took a closer look at the model of the Cullinan I. He swallowed hard and beckoned the others to join him. 'When we heard that the pavilion had been broken into, I had this strange feeling of déjà vu,' he said. 'Now I know what it reminded me of. It was like a variation of the Tower raid.'

'I don't follow you,' said Bryan.

'Just bear with me for a moment.' Paul turned to Mike. 'You've been here before. Do you know the curator of the museum?'

'Yes, I met him last year at a meeting in Jo'burg.'

'Would you please go and find him, and bring him here as soon as you can. Then I'll explain what's on my mind.'

When Mike returned with the curator several minutes later he found Paul still staring at the model of the Cullinan I. He led the curator across to the display unit and introduced him to Paul. 'This is Mr Paul Remington. He works for the Diamond Syndicate in London, and this is his son, Jason.'

'I'm sorry to trouble you,' said Paul, 'but I think I know what happened here during that break-in last week. Is it possible to have the display cabinet opened — I'd like to take a closer look at that model of the Cullinan I.'

The curator looked at Paul in surprise. 'It's only a glass model, but yes, I can get it out for you if you really insist. As you can see, there are also a lot of high-value stones and jewellery in the display. For security reasons I'll have to clear the pavilion before opening it up.'

'I assure you there's a very good reason for my request,' replied Paul. 'My colleague here, Bryan Raleigh, is a detective chief inspector from the Art and Antiques Investigation Squad of Scotland Yard — we're both in South Africa on the track of a stolen diamond, and we'd appreciate your co-operation.'

When the other members of the public had been ushered out of the pavilion, the curator hung a 'closed' sign on the door and locked it. Then he unlocked the access door to the display cabinet, reached inside and carefully lifted out the stone labelled 'Cullinan I (glass replica)'.

Paul took the stone from him and held it in the palm of his hand under the fluorescent lights of the ceiling. 'Do you see that,' he whispered to Bryan. 'Those rear facets are reflecting back the light — you can't see my hand through the stone as you would with a glass model, even when I tilt it at an angle.'

He turned to the puzzled curator. 'This is not a glass model. It's not even quartz. This is the real thing — the actual Cullinan I diamond. It was stolen from the royal sceptre in a raid on the Tower of London five years ago!'

The curator clearly thought Paul was deranged. 'But how can it be the real thing?'

'The man who broke in here last week was the master-mind behind the theft of the Cullinan I in London,' explained Paul. 'He has been operating in Cape Town as an art dealer under the name of Vandam. The Cullinan was stolen for a collector in Brazil, and when this man died recently, the diamond came back into the possession of Vandam. Five days ago, the police raided his headquarters in Cape Town, but the man escaped. It's now clear that he broke in here and substituted your glass model of the Cullinan with the real diamond.'

'But why would he do that?' asked the curator.

'We were close on his tail, and he wanted a safe place to hide it while he made arrangements to leave the country. What safer place could he find than your Diamond Pavilion!'

Out of the corner of his eye, Paul saw a man looking in through the window of the locked door to the pavilion. The man was heavily built, and Paul could see the light glinting from his bald dome.

Paul turned so that his back was to the door. 'Don't look round now, but the man we are hunting, Leo Vandam, is looking at us from the doorway.' He handed the Cullinan back to the curator. 'Put the diamond in your pocket without him seeing it — you can lock it up in your safe later.'

Then Paul took the CZ replica of the Cullinan out of his own pocket and slipped it to the curator. 'This is the replica that was found mounted in the royal sceptre. Vandam is still watching us, so I want you to turn slightly towards the door and make a show of giving it to me. I want him to think you've given me the diamond from the display — that will make him follow me when we leave here.'

The curator did as he was instructed, and Paul took the replica from him and put it in his pocket. When he turned back to the door, Vandam had disappeared.

The four men escorted the curator to his office and watched while he locked the big diamond in his safe. 'Get the police here as soon as you can,' said Paul. He turned to the others. 'We'd better get across to the coffee shop and pick up the girls — they may be in danger with Vandam on the loose.'

When they arrived at the cafe, they found Christine and Stephanie sitting at one of the tables.

'Where's Melanie,' asked Mike.

'She's gone back to the Big Hole,' said Christine. 'She wanted to copy down the figures on the display board.' Then she saw the expression of alarm on Mike's face. 'Why, what's the matter?'

'She could be in danger — Leo Vandam's here. We've found the Cullinan — Vandam had planted it in the Diamond Pavilion,' said Paul. 'The museum curator is phoning for the police, so I want you and Steffi to join him in the admin office while we locate Melanie.'

'Let's go,' said Jason and set off running through the streets of old buildings in the direction of the viewing platform with Mike, Paul and Bryan hot on his heels. As they turned the last corner they heard a scream. Thirty yards ahead they saw Vandam dragging Melanie away from the platform towards the unfenced perimeter of the Big Hole.

'Let the girl go, Vandam,' Mike shouted.

Leo spun round and pulled a forty-five calibre automatic from his shoulder holster. He held the muzzle to Melanie's head. Back off, all of you, or the girl dies,' he growled. He looked over his shoulder and edged backwards toward a roped-off section of the Big Hole and a sign that read 'Danger — Unfenced Boundary — Keep Out'. He grabbed Melanie round the waist with his left arm, lifted her bodily in the air and stepped over the rope barrier. He took a few more paces until he was standing at the perimeter of the mine and turned back to face the four men.

'Let me handle this,' said Paul. He turned and faced Leo. 'It's no good Vandam — let her go.'

'Which of you has the big diamond?' snarled Leo.

Paul stepped forward and pulled the CZ replica out of his pocket. 'I'm Paul Remington.' He held the stone up for Leo to see. 'Put the girl down, Vandam, you can't win this one.'

Leo laughed grimly. 'So at last we meet face to face, Mr Remington. And once again you interfere with my plans. However, I am a reasonable man, so I make you an offer. You take five steps towards me and put the diamond down on the ground. I will pick it up and release the young lady.'

Paul stepped over the rope barrier. 'Sorry, Leo. I have a better plan. You lay down your gun and release the girl now.'

Leo's face turned scarlet with anger. 'Stay where you are, or I kill the girl.' He brandished the gun at Paul.

Paul raised a hand in surrender. 'OK Vandam — you win. Here's your precious diamond.' He tossed the CZ replica high in the air. As the stone sailed out above Leo's head, he dropped the gun and stretched up to catch the gem, his hand closing on empty air as the Cullinan replica fell out of his reach into the gaping cavern of the mine. Leo gave a strangled cry and twisted round to watch the stone as it fell. For a split second he teetered on the edge of the Big Hole, then the ground under his feet gave way and he slid backwards dragging Melanie with him.

Jason screamed and raced forward to the edge of the hole followed by the three men. Looking down he could see Leo sliding away from him on the friable shale, his hands digging into the loose earth as he attempted to slow his descent. There was no sign of Melanie, and for a heart-stopping moment Jason thought she was gone. Then he caught sight of her just below him clinging on with both hands to the branch of a small bush growing on the sloping side of the mine. Jason lay down at the edge of the hole, and inched himself forward on his stomach.

He looked over his shoulder and shouted to Paul. 'Hang on to my feet — I'll try to reach her.' With Mike and Bryan acting as anchor men at the top, Paul lowered Jason down until he was within a few inches of the terrified girl. Her right hand was nearly within reach, but the other one was too far to the left.

'I can't hang on much longer,' she gasped. 'My hands are losing their grip.'

'It's OK, Melanie, I've nearly got you.' Jason strained forward. 'I'm going to grab your right wrist first. As soon as I've got a good grip on it I want you to let go of the branch with that hand. Then we'll pull you up a few inches and I'll be able to reach your other hand.'

Melanie nodded and gritted her teeth. Jason swung his body to the left and caught hold of Melanie's right wrist. 'OK — I've got you.' He looked back over his shoulder at Paul. 'Can you pull me back a few inches?'

Paul nodded. 'We'll try, but the ground under us is beginning to give way.'

Mike and Bryan were each hanging on to one of Paul's feet and were lying flat with their legs angled wide to spread the load. They dug their feet into the loose soil and began to pull back against the combined weight of both Jason and Melanie. Almost immediately the unstable ground at the edge of the hole started to cascade down onto the two young people. Melanie ducked her head and screamed as a shower of small stones stung her arms and face.

'Stop!' shouted Jason in alarm. He blinked the dirt from his eyes and tightened his grip on the girl's right wrist. 'I'm going to try something else, Melanie,' he gasped. 'See if you can get some purchase on the ground with your toes. When I give the word, start scrabbling like mad with both feet. Then let go of the bush and reach up for my right hand. Are you ready?'

Melanie looked up at him and grimaced. 'If Paul finds he can't take our combined weight, I want you to let go of me, Jason,' she cried.

'No way, my love — now let's get you up.' Jason dug his knees into the loose soil and pulled up hard with his left arm. At the same time Melanie kicked down with both feet as she desperately tried to find to a toe-hold. Her hand lost its grip on the bush, and for an agonising moment she swung free over the Big Hole with Jason taking her full weight.

Just as he felt that his arm was about to be pulled out of its socket, Melanie's left foot found the edge of a projecting rock. She pushed up hard against the rock and Jason caught hold of her outstretched left hand. Paul felt the shock of the extra weight on his arm muscles. 'Pull now,' he called out to Mike and Bryan, and between them they slowly dragged Jason and Melanie back over the top.

Jason wrapped his arms round the shivering girl. 'You're safe now,' he whispered and held her tight.

While they were all still recovering from their exertions, they heard a shout for help from below. Paul, Mike and Bryan ran back to the edge of the mine. Looking down past the shrubs they could see Leo far below entangled in the branches of a tree which had stopped his fall at the very edge of the vertical section of the mine shaft.

Then they realised that the tree was starting to sag under his weight as its roots lost their grip on the loose soil. Suddenly the tree tore free, and with a despairing cry Leo was flung out into the void, his body spiralling down like a rag doll. A few seconds later they saw the splash as he hit the water. They gazed down in silence for a moment, half expecting to see Leo re-appear, but there was nothing except an ever-widening series of ripples spreading out over the dark waters of the Big Hole.

* * *

Mike and Jason supported the trembling Melanie between them, and followed by Paul and Bryan they walked her back towards the curator's office. Halfway there they met the Kimberley police. Melanie was clearly suffering from shock, so Mike persuaded them to give her time to recover before they questioned her.

When they arrived at the curator's office they were met by an anxious Christine and Stephanie. Paul quickly told them what had happened at the mine shaft. 'She's had a narrow escape, but she'll be OK.'

Mike sat Melanie down on a chair and then sent Jason off to organise a cup of hot sweet tea for her. While the cuts and bruises on her arms and legs were being treated by Christine and Stephanie, Melanie shivered and looked up at Mike. 'Did Paul really throw the Cullinan diamond into the Big Hole?' she whispered.

Mike bent down and put his arm around her. 'No, that was the CZ replica — Paul discovered that Leo had hidden the real stone in the Diamond Pavilion's main display cabinet. When Leo arrived at the pavilion, he saw the curator hand Paul what he thought was the Cullinan.'

After the police had questioned everyone, Bryan took the sergeant in charge to one side. 'Is there any chance that Vandam could have survived that fall?'

The sergeant shook his head. 'From that height, the effect of his velocity as he hit the water would probably have been enough to kill him — it would have been like hitting a concrete slab.'

* * *

Paul and Bryan's jubilation at recovering the Cullinan diamond was short-lived. They had not allowed for the attitude of the South African police, who insisted on taking charge of the famous diamond while they prepared and filed their report on the incident. They also arranged for one of the leading Kimberley jewellers to inspect the stone and confirm it was a diamond.

In desperation, Paul made a phone call to Sir James in London. 'I'm calling from Kimberley. We've recovered the Phantom Diamond...'

'That's great news Paul — my congratulations,' interrupted Sir James. 'When are you bringing it back?'

'Well, sir, that was the good news. The bad news is the police have impounded the stone while they're filing their report. The whole thing has got rather complicated with the death of one of Vandam's operatives in Cape Town — Leo Vandam is also dead. I'll fill you in with the details later. Right now I need you to pull a few strings and get the diamond released to me.'

'Don't worry, Paul, I'll get on to that right away.'

'One other thing. I had to come clean on the identity of the Phantom Diamond or the curator of the Diamond Pavilion would never have believed me. The police here also know the stone is a real diamond. If the theft of the Cullinan is to be kept as a state secret, and not splashed on headlines all over the South African papers tomorrow, you'll also have to insist on a secrecy clamp being imposed by the people at the top.'

'I'll get the PM to speak to the South African president immediately.'

It took another twenty-four hours before the Cullinan diamond was safely in Paul's possession. Sir James contacted the prime minister, who then had a long telephone conversation with the South African president and explained the complicated series of events which started with the raid on the Tower of London and ended at the Kimberley Open Mine Museum. The president then spoke to his police commissioner, who finally telephoned the police inspector in Kimberley.

While Paul and party were awaiting the outcome of the negotiations, they decided to use the time to visit Kimberley's McGreggor Museum and inspect its display of mineral specimens. After that, Melanie, now recovered from her ordeal, took them to the western end of the town to see an old neglected graveyard she had discovered on a previous visit.

Among the overgrown graves there were headstone inscriptions dating back to Kimberley's diamond rush days. Several of these headstones marked the burial places of young men in their early twenties and bore the simple epitaph 'Killed by a fall of reef'. Even more poignant were the smaller stones marking the graves of very young children who had 'Died of a fever' in the days when Africa was often the white man's graveyard. In her capacity of guide, Melanie then took them to the Kimberley curio shop. This was a popular venue for both tourists and local people purchasing the various medical and love potions on offer — and, when they could afford them, crocodile teeth and the mummified hands of monkeys. Some of these strange objects, Melanie explained, were the essential African talismans to ward off the evil Tokoloshi man-eater.

By the end of the day, the local press had become aware of the dramatic happenings at the Big Hole. The following morning, the Diamond Fields Advertiser printed a banner headline across its front page 'Mystery death at Open Mine Museum', and followed this with a speculative report which attempted to link the earlier break-in at the Diamond Pavilion with the gun-wielding man who had held a young girl hostage, and had then fallen to his death in the flood waters of the Big Hole.

When the Cullinan I was eventually handed over with due ceremony to Paul the following morning, he and Bryan decided to return immediately to Cape Town and then take the evening flight to the UK, leaving Stephanie and Jason to return home at their leisure. As they waved goodby that evening at Cape Town Airport, Paul noticed that Melanie and Jason were holding hands. 'Looks as if those two are more than just good friends now.'

'They make a fine pair,' answered Bryan. 'And, after all, he did save her life.'

When the SAA Boeing 777 took off on its eleven-hour flight to Heathrow, Paul breathed a sigh of relief. He tilted his seat back and patted the briefcase chained to his left wrist. His fingers checked the contours of the big diamond through the soft leather. 'You'll soon be back where you belong,' he murmured and closed his eyes. He felt drained after the events of the last few days and was soon fast asleep.

At his side Bryan was already asleep and dreaming he was back in his familiar office and wearing his comfortable old woolly cardigan.

CHAPTER 22

SOUTH AFRICA — LONDON
Thursday 7 October, 1999

After Paul and Bryan left Cape Town for the UK, Stephanie and Jason spent their last few days in South Africa at the Pretoria home of Mike and Christine. Jason had made full use of his extra time with Melanie, and they had spent the hours together swimming, sun-bathing, and making plans for the future. Just before they finally parted at the barrier in Johannesburg's International Airport, he took her on one side.

'I'm not very good with words, but I want you to know that every morning I'll be crossing one more day off my calender until you're back in the UK for good.'

Melanie fought back a tear and kissed him. 'Farewell, my love. I'll expect a regular letter from you until then.'

Christine, Stephanie and Mike, who had been talking among themselves and trying to ignore the tender scene of separation between Jason and Melanie, smiled knowingly at each other as they too made their farewells. Then Stephanie and Jason went through into passport control and joined the other passengers taking the direct flight back to London.

* * *

When Paul had arrived back in his office earlier in the week, his secretary Debbie was as glad to see him as Sir James was in dispensing with her services. Sir James was a creature of habit, and hated any disturbance to his normal daily routine. Today, when Stephanie placed his cup of coffee on his desk at the appointed time, with no sugar and just the right amount of cream, he felt that stability had been restored to his world at last. He picked up his phone and summoned Paul and Steven to his office.

When they arrived, he sat back and smiled at both of them. 'Now that the Cullinan I has been restored to its rightful place in the royal sceptre, I want to take this opportunity of thanking both of you for your part in its recovery.'

Steven looked uncomfortable. 'I'm afraid my involvement was pretty minor, Sir James.'

'Nonsense, your initial contact with DCI Raleigh, and your subsequent investigation into the death of the Tower of London warden, were most useful. You also managed the Special Operations Department in Paul's absence with, I must add, your usual flair. They also serve, who only man the office.'

Sir James sipped his coffee appreciatively, and then looked at Paul. 'I have just heard from the prime minister that he is putting your name forward, together with those of DCI Raleigh and your Pretoria friend Mike Reece, in the Queen's birthday honours list. I understand, unofficially of course, that each of you will be in line for an OBE for services rendered to the crown.'

Sir James caught the brief flicker of disappointment that passed across Steven's face. 'I have also heard that you, Steven, can expect an MBE in the same connection.' He paused for a moment and then turned to Paul. 'There are still two things concerning the Phantom Diamond affair that I find confusing. Tell me, how did you get hold of the information connecting Vandam to Perez senior, and what finally led you to Kimberley?'

It was Paul's turn to look uncomfortable. 'I have to confess, Sir James, that it was my son Jason who suggested we should use the computer expertise of Mike Reece's daughter Melanie, and interrogate Vandam's computer files to obtain the information.'

Sir James squinted at Paul through his gold-rimmed glasses in mock concern. 'I believe that is called hacking, and is unlawful.'

Paul nodded. 'At the time, I considered the ends justified the means.'

'In the circumstances, I have to agree with you. One of these days you must introduce me to young Melanie. I still remember the occasion when she was kidnapped, together with your wife, after you had got proof of the Soviet involvement in the Peking Diamond affair. That and the business at the Big Hole is the second time a Russian has put her life in danger. I understand your son Jason rescued her on that occasion — you must be very proud of him. But I digress — you still haven't explained your reason for the Kimberley visit.'

Paul smiled. 'That was a pure hunch. I think I must have subconsciously linked the Tower raid, in which nothing appeared to be stolen, with the Diamond Pavilion break-in, where once again nothing seemed to have gone missing.'

The answer seemed to satisfy Sir James. He got up from behind his desk and shook hands with Paul and Jason. 'The PM and the Queen are both delighted at the successful return of the diamond, which, I must remind you, never went missing as far as the general public are concerned. The home secretary and the commissioner of police are equally relieved that a national scandal, which could have resulted in their resignation, has been averted. Now we can all look forward, I hope, to a period of relative calm before Christmas. Then, in March, there will be the coronation in Westminster Abbey. The two of you, together with DCI Raleigh, Mr Reece, and your respective wives and offspring, will be receiving invitations to the ceremony as part of the Royal Family's recognition of your services.'

When Paul and Steven returned to their office, Debbie made them each a cup of coffee. 'You both look rather smug,' she said. 'I take it you're in Sir James's good books at the moment.'

'Yes, you're right,' said Paul. 'But I still find it a bit unnerving when he smiles at me. And tell me Steven, what was all that waffle he spouted about you managing the department in my absence with your usual flair?'

'I think he was referring to the time I stopped some yobbos from denting his Daimler.'

Paul laughed. 'Well one thing's for sure, we'll both have to behave ourselves until after March 16, or our awards and invitations will be cancelled.'

Steven winked at Debbie. 'At times like this I'm glad I'm still single — Stephanie and Jason would make Paul's life a misery if that happened.'

Debbie looked curious. 'What's all that about awards — is the Queen going to give you both a knighthood?' Steven put his finger to his lips. 'It's confidential, but next year you may have to curtsy to us before you take dictation, or at least sit on my knee.'

When Debbie had left the office, Paul looked sternly at Steven. 'You've made her blush again. I know it's common gossip you've had your way with most of the diamond sorting staff, but why don't you ask Debbie out for a change? She's a nice mature thirty-eight, and she knows all your funny ways by now.'

Steven pulled a face. 'You sound just like my mother.'

'I just don't see why you shouldn't suffer like the rest of us happily marrieds,' grinned Paul, 'and you'll need a partner to take with you to the Christmas dinner dance.'

CHAPTER 23

LONDON
Thursday 16 March, 2000

Coronation day dawned bright and clear, to the relief of the nation's weather forecasters and the many planners. For weeks Parliament Square and the precincts of Westminster Abbey had echoed to the sounds of drilling and hammering as the ornate Royal Entrance and Annex was erected at the Abbey's west front. A similar scene of frantic activity had occurred along the Mall from Trafalgar Square to the statue of Queen Victoria in front of Buckingham Palace as a series of arches, surmounted with gigantic crowns, were erected.

In keeping with the futuristic theme of the country's millennium celebrations, the newly crowned sovereign was going to appear on the balcony of Buckingham Palace that evening and switch on twenty high-power lasers mounted on Admiralty Arch. These would create an elevated tunnel of light all the way down the Mall to Victoria's statue, where reflectors had been placed to fan the laser beams out into the night sky over the Palace.

The choice of mid-March for the Coronation had been a difficult one, and was affected by the desire to place the ceremony within the context of the first few months of the millennium celebrations, and yet to move it away from the worst period of the winter weather. Some of King William V's more elderly advisers remembered with a shiver the low temperatures, the pelting rain, and the storm clouds that had accompanied his grandmother's coronation on the second of June forty-seven years ago.

Although the forecasters predicted daytime temperatures around ten degrees celsius, the thousands of spectators, who had camped out overnight along the route to be taken by the royal procession, were experiencing a very chilly dawn as they slowly emerged from their cocoons of rugs and sleeping bags.

Just before seven o'clock in the morning, an hour before the first procession was due to leave the Mansion House, the crowds packed around Parliament Square watched the ermine-dressed groups of peers and their ladies arriving at the Peer's Entrance to the Abbey. They were instructed to be in their seats between seven and eight o'clock that morning — the doors of the Abbey would be closed at eight-thirty. The whole of the ground floor of the Abbey's south transept had been allocated to peers, and the corresponding area in the north transept to peeresses, the seats on both sides rising gently in tiers as in a theatre. Above the peers, in a specially constructed 'dress circle', were seats for members of the Houses of Parliament and other dignitaries, and these groups were beginning to file in from a separate entrance.

Outside the Abbey, in a stand immediately above the Peer's Entrance, members of the public were huddled together in coats and headscarves. As they watched the arrival of the various dignitaries, many ate an early breakfast of sandwiches, and tried to keep warm with cups of tea dispensed from thermos flasks.

Equally early to arrive at the Abbey from their Regents Park flat were Paul, Stephanie and Jason Remington. Not far behind them were Mike, Christine and Melanie Reece, who had flown in from South Africa two days previously, and were staying in their Cheyne Walk apartment overlooking the Thames. Steven Heming had spent the night with Bryan Raleigh in his Covent Garden home, and this morning they had both decided to walk to the Abbey because of the congested streets. All eight of them had tickets for seats in the nave of the Abbey in an area reserved for 'distinguished members of the public'. After some forty minutes in a slow moving queue, they arrived high up in the balcony on the south side of the nave, and found they were all sitting together in the same row.

Jason swapped seats with his mother so he could sit beside Melanie. 'This is rather fun,' he said, 'but will we be able to see much from here?'

'We'll just have to share the binoculars when the royal procession arrives in the nave,' said Paul. He pointed to his left. 'Once the processions have passed through the nave, we'll be able to watch the main ceremony on that big projection screen. The acoustics are good so we should be able to hear the ceremony reasonably well.'

Christine looked at her coronation programme. 'I see there are four processions due to arrive at the Abbey before King Edward's royal procession. The lord mayor's one is first at eight-thirty, that's followed by a motor-car procession of the junior members of the royal family at nine-fifteen; representatives of foreign states arrive ten minutes later, and a procession of the speaker of the house of commons half an hour after that.'

Mike turned up his coat collar, and rubbed his hands together. 'By that time I'll be a block of ice. It's all very well for you hardy locals, but we've just come from South Africa and temperatures up in the thirties.'

'I thought you might go down with hypothermia this morning,' said Stephanie, 'so I've brought two thermos jugs of coffee laced with brandy.'

'A few more hours here and that could be a life saver,' said Christine, pulling her coat over her knees.' She pointed to someone in the seats far below them. 'That looks like Sir James.'

'Yes, you're right,' agreed Paul. 'He's wearing a smart pinstriped suit, just like Bryan's.' Paul lowered his voice, 'I half expected Bryan to wear his woolly cardigan in this temperature.'

While they were patiently awaiting the arrival of the lord mayor's procession, Jason pulled a small cardboard box from his pocket and gave it to Melanie.

'What's this?' she asked, removing the lid and lifting out a small round object wrapped in tissue paper.

'It's something I picked up in Austria on holiday two years ago — unwrap it.'

Melanie undid the tissue paper and picked out an embossed silver ring. 'Oh, that's lovely, Jason — can I keep it?'

'It's an Austrian engagement ring. After what we said to each other last year, I want you to wear it as a sort of token. Will you do that for me, Melanie?'

'I'd be proud to Jason — that's a sweet idea.' She turned and kissed him on the cheek.

Jason blushed. 'Steady on, Melanie,' he murmured. 'They could shove us both in the Tower for snogging in the Abbey.'

At that moment there were sounds of activity outside the west door of the Abbey. Steven suddenly realised that Bryan had fallen asleep at his side, and prodded him awake. The first of the four processions had arrived, and they were at last able to see and identify some of the distinguished members who filed in from the west door of the Abbey and passed down the length of the nave to their seats. The lord mayor, heads of foreign states and members of parliament were all seated out of sight in the choir and in the transepts, but Paul and his group were able to identify many of them from the television picture in the balcony. At one point, the television camera zoomed in to show King William's mother, Princess Diana, seated in the front row of the balcony above the royal box.

Melanie turned to her mother, 'So she *is* here — when we listened to the Queen's 1998 Christmas message, we wondered if Charles and Diana would both be present at William's coronation.'

'Well, at least they don't have to sit together,' said Christine. 'I still find it very sad that things didn't work out between them. Just think — today we might have been sitting here watching King Charles' coronation, with his consort, Diana, at his side.'

Shortly before the arrival of King William V, they saw the procession of the princes and princesses of the royal blood pass down the nave and across the transept to the royal box on the south side of the coronation chair. They were followed by Elizabeth the Queen Mother, Prince Philip, and their immediate family. The interior of the Abbey was now ablaze with colour. On the big television screen in the balcony they could make out the scarlet robes of the Lords, the green, blue and scarlet mantles of the Orders of Chivalry, the full-dress military and diplomatic uniforms, the embroidered cloaks of the clergy, the exotic costumes of the foreign dignitaries, and the heralds in their quartered tabards.

Finally, the big moment had arrived for all the spectators as the abbey beadle entered the west door followed by the royal chaplains in scarlet, the representatives of the churches of

England, Wales and Scotland, the Dean of Westminster, the Archbishop of Canterbury, and the Archbishop of York. At last, the slim figure of seventeen year old King William came into view, clad in a richly embroidered crimson cloak over a plain white silk shirt and white satin breeches. At the appearance of the King, the entire congregation inside the Abbey rose to its feet.

When the royal procession had passed out of sight through the ornately carved choir screen into the transept, the eyes of all those sitting in the nave returned to the television screen. They saw the King climb the four steps to the 'theatre' area of the transept, and walk past his throne. He paused briefly as he came to the royal box and acknowledged his mother sitting in the balcony above.

The first section of the coronation culminated in the ceremony of recognition in which the Archbishop of Canterbury presented King William to the assembled peers, peeresses and dignitaries. The King took the royal oath, and this was followed by a communion service. After the service, the King rose to his feet, and the crimson robe was unfastened and lifted from his shoulders by the Lord Chamberlain. They saw him sit clad in his white silk shirt and white satin breeches in the King Edward's coronation chair in front of the high altar.

Mike drew Melanie's attention to the television screen. 'You can just see the Scottish Stone of Scone under the wooden seat of the chair. King Edward III, who was nicknamed the Hammer of the Scots, brought the stone back to London from north of the border.'

A canopy of silk was held over the King while the archbishop anointed his sovereign's hands, breast and head with consecrated oil from the eagle-shaped ampulla held by the Dean of Westminster. The sovereign was then dressed in the richly embroidered imperial robe. Next, the keeper of the Jewel House presented the King's ring to the archbishop who placed it on the fourth finger of the sovereign's right hand. A fleeting close-up of the ring on the television screen showed the cross of St. George set in rubies across a large blue sapphire surrounded by small diamonds.

'I bet the VIPs can't see that sort of detail,' Christine whispered to Mike.

Then the archbishop placed the royal sceptre in the King's right hand, and the rod in his left hand. Finally, with everyone in the Abbey rising to their feet, the Dean of Westminster picked up the St. Edward's crown from the altar and carried it to the archbishop. After holding the crown high over the head of the King, the archbishop slowly lowered it and placed it securely on the sovereign's head. The peers and peeresses had waited, their coronets poised in the air, for this moment of acclamation. A great shout went up, as in unison they donned their own golden circlets. The trumpets sounded a fanfare, and then they heard the cannons being fired in salute from the Tower of London.

The final act of pageantry was about to begin to the strains of the national anthem. With the beefeaters — the traditional yeomen of the guard — lining each side of the nave, King William emerged from the chapel holding the sceptre in his right hand and the orb in his left hand. Escorting him were the Archbishop of Canterbury and the Dean of Westminster, and with a line of ten gentlemen at arms on each side, the plumes on their burnished helmets swaying as they kept step with him, he walked slowly in procession down the nave towards the west door of the Abbey.

When King William V, his serious young face flushed with pride, passed beneath Paul and his group sitting high in the balcony section of the nave, Jason pointed at the royal sceptre the King was holding in his right hand. 'There goes the Phantom Diamond,' he whispered.

'A phantom no more, I'm glad to say,' exclaimed Paul with feeling. 'I wonder if he's aware of the adventures that diamond has had since his grandmother held the sceptre at her own coronation in 1953.'

'Stolen from the Jewel House, hidden in a collector's safe in Brazil for five years, sent to South Africa to be sliced up, fought over in Kimberley, and, at long last, restored to the royal sceptre just before a coronation,' said Bryan. 'That would take a bit of believing even in a novel. Perhaps it's just as well the history of the Phantom Diamond has been classified as a state secret.'

Melanie looked thoughtfully at Jason and touched the silver ring on her finger. 'You and King William are almost the same age. I had quite a crush on him once, you know. But there's no way I'd want to swap you for him, my love. After all, it was you who saved my life at the Big Hole. What with that, and your father rescuing me from the clutches of those Russian thugs when I was only three, you probably think I'm accident prone.'

'It had crossed my mind,' replied Jason. He took Melanie's hand and kissed it. 'Despite that, I'm still willing to act as your minder — from now till death us do part — and I've just thought of a great way you can reward me for my services!'

Aware of her parents' sudden interest in the conversation, Melanie winked at Jason. 'You're always welcome to play with my computer,' she replied with a smile.

By now the tail end of the King's procession had passed out of the nave, and was being followed by the Queen Mother and Prince Philip, their immediate family, and the princes and princesses of the royal blood. Then the archbishops, the clergy and the heads of foreign states started moving along the nave to join their coaches and cars lined up outside the annex.

Paul looked across at Mike, Bryan and Steven. 'If we get separated when we leave the Abbey, don't forget you're all invited back to our place for the rest of the day. We've got plenty of food and drink laid on, so we can continue the celebrations while we watch tonight's television coverage of the festivities.'

* * *

It was another hour before the members of the public in the nave were able to leave the Abbey. When Paul and company eventually filed out into Parliament Square, he guided them across the crowded roads into St James Park and along Horse Guards Parade.

'I suggest we walk the half mile to Trafalgar Square and then catch the underground to Baker Street. From there we can take a stroll through Regents Park to our flat in Prince Albert Road,' he said.

The day, although still cold, was bright and sunny and they all enjoyed the chance to stretch their legs as they walked through the park and under Admiralty Arch into Trafalgar Square. They found the Square packed with sightseers. With thousands of people moving across London, it took them another hour to struggle onto a train and fight their way out again at Baker Street.

Steven mopped his brow as they all emerged into the sunlight. 'Phew, that was even worse than the rush hour — it would have been quicker to walk.'

When they finally arrived at Paul and Stephanie's third floor flat in Prince Albert Road, Jason opened the sliding glass door in the lounge and walked out onto the small balcony overlooking the northern perimeter of the Park. He beckoned Melanie to join him. 'Listen — you can just hear the shouts of the crowds along the procession route,' he said.

Melanie put her arm around Jason, and they stood there in silence looking out over the trees in the late afternoon sunshine, content to be close to each other. A few minutes later, Paul's secretary Debbie arrived and joined Steven who was helping Stephanie load a tray with plates and glasses in the kitchen. 'Thanks for inviting me over, Steffi,' she said. 'I've been glued to my TV all day — it must have been a marvellous experience actually being there in the Abbey.'

In the lounge Christine was removing cling film from plates of food, while Paul and Bryan began opening bottles of champagne. Debbie and Steven joined them and then wandered over to the balcony door where Melanie and Jason were standing.

'Hey, you two,' said Steven, 'it's our turn for a cuddle on the balcony — you're both wanted behind the bar.'

When they had all been provided with a glass of champagne and were assembled together in the lounge, Bryan held his hand up for attention. 'Now that we're all armed with a glass of bubbly, I'd like to propose a toast. Please raise your glasses to King William the Fifth. May our new young Monarch enjoy a long and happy reign.'

After the loyal toast, Jason sidled up to his mother. 'Would you and dad mind if Melanie and I went back to Buckingham Palace to see the illuminations.'

'You'll get a far better view on TV of William switching on the lights than standing in the middle of those crowds,' said Stephanie.

'Yes, I know,' replied Jason. 'But we'd like to be there and experience the atmosphere. It's something we can tell our children about.'

Stephanie smiled. 'But not for a few years yet, I hope.' She looked at her watch. 'However, if that's what you really want to do, you'd better go now. It'll be dark in an hour, and the crowds are still pretty thick around the Palace. Just make sure Melanie clears it with Mike first.'

'Thanks, mum, we'll be back around midnight — so keep the party going until then.'

* * *

Jason and Melanie walked back across Regents Park to Baker Street underground station and took a train to Piccadilly Circus and then to Hyde Park Corner. When they entered the bottom end of Constitution Hill they found it less crowded than the Mall, and by moving across into Green Park they were able to find a position on the north side of Queen Victoria's Memorial which gave them a good view of both the Buckingham Palace balcony and the thousands of people who were jammed together all the way down the Mall to the Palace gates.

By seven forty-five it was nearly dark, and the crowds around the statue of Queen Victoria started chanting 'We want the King'. A few minutes later, King William appeared on the balcony to a roar of greetings from the crowd. William was followed by the Queen Mother, Prince Philip, Prince Charles, Princess Margaret, and Anne the Princess Royal. A few seconds after that, Andrew the Prince Regent, Prince Edward, and Princess Diana with Prince Henry appeared, and there was another roar from the crowd.

A precisely eight o'clock, an equerry handed King William a small radio control unit. The King held it up at arms length so that the crowds could see the unit's flashing red button. Then he lowered it and with the index finger of his other hand he pressed the button. There was a fraction of a second delay, and then the sky above the Mall was pierced by twenty beams of alternate red and blue light from the lasers mounted on Admiralty Arch. At the same time the huge metal crowns mounted on the arches spanning the Mall came alive with hundreds of small white flashing lights. At the final arch behind Queen Victoria's statue, a group of metallic reflectors spread the laser beams out like a gigantic fan above the Palace.

Unseen by the majority of the crowd, massed army bands had assembled in the forecourt below the Palace Balcony, and they now struck up the national anthem. As the familiar strains of the music wafted out across the multitude packed in front of the Palace gates, they started singing, and then the sounds of singing slowly spread up the Mall in waves as more and more people joined in.

Melanie was so overcome by this mass demonstration of affection for the King and the royal family that she started to cry. Jason hugged her to him and kissed her wet face. 'You're not the only softie in this crowd, Melanie. Here, take my hanky.' Then, as the last echoing notes of the anthem slowly died away into the night, the laser lights were suddenly switched off, and there was a loud bang as a rocket exploded high over the Palace, its dazzling red, white and blue stars spreading out into a gigantic coloured ball of light.

A whole range of new firework spectaculars had been especially developed for the occasion, and the massive crowd were kept enthralled by the pyrotechnics for the next thirty minutes. When it was finally over, the laser lights were switched on again. Melanie smiled up at Jason. 'Now that's what I call a really unforgettable day, and one I'll remember all my life.'

Jason nodded. He took Melanie in his arms and kissed her tenderly. 'I told my mother we wanted to be part of the crowd tonight so we could tell our children about it. I take it that sentiment meets with your approval.'

Melanie fingered the silver ring on her finger. 'How could I refuse so enticing a proposition, my love.' She looked at her watch. 'But first I think we should concentrate on getting home by midnight or my fairy godmother might make all this magic disappear.'

CHAPTER 24

LONDON
Six months later — Saturday 16 September, 2000

After breakfast that morning, Jason went down to the foyer of his parent's flat in Prince Albert Road and picked up the mail. He got back in the lift, pressed the button to the third floor and idly flicked through the letters and circulars. Suddenly he froze as he recognised the address on the back of a buff-coloured envelope. By the time he arrived back in the flat he was in a state of high agitation.

'Anything interesting?' called his father from the kitchen. When Jason remained silent, Paul got up and walked into the hall. He found his son had dropped the morning's post on the floor and was tearing open a buff envelope.

Jason pulled out a typewritten sheet of paper and scanned it impatiently. Then he let out a whoop of joy. 'I've done it,' he cried, and handed the letter to Paul. 'It's a first class honours degree!'

Stephanie came out of the bedroom to see what all the noise was about and looked over Paul's shoulder as he read out Jason's exam results. Then they both linked arms with Jason and danced him around the hall in a wild jig.

'That's absolutely splendid,' panted Paul. 'Congratulations — it's great to see all your hard work has paid off at last.'

'If you still want to join the Syndicate's Research Group at Marlow, I'll ask Sir James to put in a word for you,' added Stephanie.

During the summer vacation, Jason had been employed in the Diamond Syndicate's small development department in its London Manorhouse Street headquarters with the understanding that if he obtained a good degree, there was a possible opening for him in the Marlow operation.

'Thanks, mum, I'd appreciate that,' said Jason. 'I must ring Melanie now and tell her the good news.'

While he was on the telephone, Paul pulled a face at Stephanie. 'It's just as well Mike and Christine have moved into the Cheyne Walk flat — Jason's phone calls to Pretoria were costing me a fortune.'

'Well at least they'll be able to see each other more often now. That's probably why he's been saving up his Diamond Syndicate wages all summer,' said Christine.

'I think he's planning something special for their flat-warming party tonight,' replied Paul. 'I overheard him making a phone call to Mike yesterday. It seems he's arranged to see him earlier this evening.'

Stephanie smiled. 'I've a feeling tonight's party is going to be quite a celebration.'

***

Jason arrived at the Reece's flat overlooking the Thames in Cheyne Walk, Chelsea, at six o'clock that evening. He was wearing his best suit and his auburn hair was well brushed. Mike opened the door to him. 'Good to see you, Jason — and congratulations on your degree. Come on in — the girls are still making themselves beautiful for the party.'

Jason followed Mike into the lounge and sat nervously on the edge of an easy chair. 'Now that I've got my degree,' he said, 'there's a good chance the Syndicate will offer me a job in their Marlow Research Group.'

'That sounds like a very good start for you,' agreed Mike. 'Now, what was it you wanted to see me about.'

Jason turned slightly pink and stood up. 'Well, you may have noticed how well Melanie and I have been getting on together,' began Jason.

'I think we've all been aware of that, Jason,' replied Mike with a smile.

Jason began pacing up and down the room. 'Melanie and I

have had a talk, and now that I've finished my degree course, and she has decided to stay permanently here in the UK, well we'd like to, to ...' Jason's mouth dried up and he ground to a halt.

'To get engaged?' prompted Mike.

Jason cleared his throat. 'Would that be alright with you and Christine?'

'We'd both be very proud to have you as a future son-in-law Jason. But of course you'll have to show me your bank balance first — I can't let my daughter become engaged to a pauper.'

'I'm sorry, I should have thought of that. My funds are a bit low at the moment — I've just bought Melanie an engagement ring,' stammered Jason.

Mike laughed. 'Relax, Jason, I was only joking. So you've bought the ring. Well we mustn't waste it. If I know Melanie, she'll be dying to wear it at the earliest possible moment. I think the best plan is for me to make the formal announcement of your engagement at the party this evening. Would that be agreeable to you both?'

'Well, yes — but don't you want to discuss it with Christine first?'

'Between you and me, Jason, I think she's already got a pretty good idea of your intentions. Now sit down, take it easy, and let me pour you a drink.'

* * *

The apartment that Mike's maiden aunt Muriel had left him in her will was spacious with a large balcony overlooking the Thames. The apartment block had been built in the early 1900s. Although it had the high ceilings of the period, it also had the original antique plumbing, and Mike had already engaged the services of a builder to install a modern central heating system and to fit out a new bathroom and kitchen. For the flat-warming party that evening, Christine had laid up a buffet supper in the dining room for their guests, and Mike had set up a bar with Melanie's help in the kitchen.

Paul and Stephanie were the first to arrive and were served drinks on the balcony by Melanie.

'How did Jason's meeting with Mike go this afternoon?' whispered Stephanie.

Melanie giggled. 'Mum and I were listening at the door — poor Jason dried up and had to be prompted by dad. But it's all official now, and Jason's let me wear his ring.' She proudly displayed the deep blue Thai sapphire surrounded by small diamonds.

The next guest to arrive was Bryan, carrying two bottles of champagne. 'I thought you might be needing reinforcements,' he said handing them over to Jason. 'Paul has just told me the good news of your exam results, and I notice that Melanie's wearing a rather lovely ring, so perhaps two congratulations are in order.'

'Thanks — and top marks for the detective work,' said Jason. 'If you go through onto the balcony, Melanie will serve you an aperitif.'

A few minutes later, Steven and Debbie arrived. Steven looked around the assembled party. 'Sorry we're a bit late — I'm not very good at bow ties, and nor is Debbie — but she does have other hidden assets.' He handed Melanie two bottles of wine. 'Some 1994 Buiten Blanc to remind you of the Cape.'

Mike and Paul were reminiscing over their drinks in a corner of the lounge. 'Do you remember that dinner party your aunt Muriel gave us all back in 1981,' said Paul.

'That was quite an evening,' agreed Mike, 'and at the end she gave us that hilarious recital on her grand piano.' He pointed to the piano at the far end of the room. 'We've still got the instrument, although neither of us can play it — we kept it as a sort of memorial to her.'

'She had some controversial views about marriage. I remember her approving of Stephanie and myself because we were flaunting convention and living together.'

Just then they heard the entry phone buzzer. Melanie answered it and operated the remote door latch in the lobby below. A few minutes later she opened the front door to Sir James. 'Good evening, my dear, you must be Michael Reece's daughter Melanie,' said Sir James.

'That's right,' answered Melanie with a smile. 'Please come in, Sir James. You know Paul and Stephanie of course. Steven and

Debbie are also here, and so is Bryan Raleigh of Scotland Yard. But first of all, let me introduce you to my mother and father.'

While Sir James was talking to Mike and Christine, Melanie invited everyone to help themselves to the buffet dinner laid out in the dining room. Some time later when they had all eaten, Paul signalled for Steven to start opening the bottles of champagne. One of the corks flew across the room and a cheer went up when Sir James managed to field it. Melanie took the opened bottles from Steven, and started filling a tray-full of glasses. When she had finished, Jason acted as wine waiter and served them around the room.

Sir James took a glass from Jason as he passed by. 'Paul has just told me the good news of your exam results. Congratulations, we must have a talk together soon. I'll ask Stephanie to make an appointment.'

'Thank you, Sir James, I'd really appreciate your help and advice,' said Jason.

Paul tapped his glass with his fingernail. 'Can I have your attention for a moment, ladies and gentlemen. First of all I would like you to drink a toast with me to Christine and Mike, and to wish them a long and happy retirement in this delightful apartment.' Paul paused while they raised their glasses to their hosts, and then continued. 'You may have noticed the two young people who have been plying you with drink tonight — but have any of you spotted the ring on the third finger of the young lady's left hand.'

Melanie held up her left hand for all to see.

'For the benefit of those who have not already made the connection,' said Paul, 'this seems the ideal moment for Stephanie and myself to proudly announce the engagement of our son Jason, to Melanie, the daughter of Christine and Mike. Will you please raise your glasses again and drink to their future happiness together.'

Paul paused again while the two young people were being congratulated. 'Before, I sit down and shut up, I'm going to say a few words to the newly engaged couple.'

'Time to leave,' Steven whispered to Debbie. 'Paul's going to make a speech!'

'I heard that, Steven,' laughed Paul. 'I just want to say that for us old fogeys it's encouraging to see engagements and marriages coming back into fashion again. From the seventies onwards, three out of four couples living together didn't bother to make these formal commitments to each other. Now it seems the wheel has turned full circle. Finally, I want to remind Jason and Melanie that being in love with each other is not enough. They must also be prepared to temper their love with tolerance and understanding, and so shape their future together that when they look back on their lives it will be with pride and not regret.'

'Hear, hear,' cried Steven, and started clapping vigorously to prevent Paul from saying any more.

Later that evening, Jason and Melanie stood on the balcony together looking out at the lights reflecting from the surface of the Thames.

The night was warm and clear, and a crescent moon had just appeared from behind the slowly drifting clouds. Melanie put her arms around Jason. 'That was sweet of your father to offer those few words of advice to us.'

Jason smiled and kissed her on the nose. 'I must admit it made me think of that film "Arsenic and Old Lace" we saw on the TV — you know, the scene at the beginning where the girl is being chased by Cary Grant and says, "But I want you to love me for my mind as well".'

'And he replies, "One thing at a time!",' laughed Melanie.

'Seriously though, I know what my father was getting at,' said Jason, frowning. 'Up until Kimberley last year I was worried that our affair was going almost too smoothly — our parents had to go through some very testing events before they finally got married. I still dream about that time at the Big Hole. But in the dream it's Leo and not you that I find hanging onto that bush, and I wake up in a sweat calling out your name.'

Melanie brushed back the auburn hair that had fallen across Jason's forehead. 'Nearly losing each other certainly clarifies one's priorities in life,' she murmured. 'I'll never forget the feeling of relief when you got hold of me just as I was giving up hope. I knew then you'd never let me go — even if we'd both fallen to our death.'

For a moment, Jason's emotions were almost too much for him. He took Melanie's left hand in his and kissed her fingers tenderly. 'I see you're still wearing the silver Austrian ring.'

'Now we're engaged, my love, I'm wearing it as your token for a wedding ring.'

Jason sighed. 'If this is all a dream, promise never to wake me up.' Her perfume invaded his senses as it had done the first time they made love, and he took her in his arms and kissed her. 'I'm not in favour of a long engagement,' he whispered, his fingers caressing the cluster of blond curls which hung above the soft curve of her neck. 'After I've seen Sir James and clinched that job at Marlow, I suggest we start thinking seriously about getting married and setting up home together.'

'Oh yes, I'd really like that,' agreed Melanie. 'And when you see Sir James, you can put in a good word for me as well — I'm sure the Syndicate's Marlow group could use a computer programmer, and I'd love a nice little town house by the Thames.'

Jason smiled at her eagerness. 'A new monarch, a new millennium and a new life together — now that can't be bad.'

Melanie's cornflower blue eyes twinkled. 'You haven't tried my cooking yet!'

Glossary

Brilliant cut	The most often used cut for diamonds, this consists of 57 facets (plus a culet, a small facet sometimes polished on the pointed end of the pavilion to safeguard it from damage). There are 33 crown facets (including the central 'table' facet) and 24 pavilion facets. Variants of the round brilliant cut are the marquise, the oval, and the pear-shape, all of which have 57 facets.
Brillianteerer	The skilled diamond polisher who takes the partly finished diamond from the cross-worker, polishes the final sequence of 24 crown and 16 pavilion facets and gives all the facets their final finishing polish.
Bruter	The craftsman who specialises in producing the rounded or fancy-shape (e.g. pear shape), girdle of a polished diamond.
Carat	A unit of weight for gemstones. The metric carat was standardised as a fifth of a gram in 1914. The carat is divided into four 'grains' as a measure for pearls and small rough diamonds, and into one-hundred 'points' as a measure for small polished diamonds.
Cleavage	A property possessed by some gemstones (particularly diamond) which enables them to be divided, or 'cleaved' along a plane of weak atomic or molecular bonding.

Cleaver	The skilled member of a diamond polishing workshop who cuts a groove or 'kerf' parallel with the diamond's cleavage plane and then inserts a cleaving blade in the kerf and applies a sharp blow to part the stone in two.
Cross-worker	The skilled diamond polisher who grinds the table facet, and the sixteen main crown and pavilion facets on a brilliant-cut stone.
Crown	That portion of any faceted gemstone above the stone's perimeter or 'girdle'.
Diamantaire	Diamond cutter or dealer.
Dop	A device for holding a gemstone during bruting, sawing or faceting. It may be as simple as a metal cup (for bruting, mounted on the end of a wooden rod or stick) in which the stone is cemented, or, in the case of a diamond, soldered.
Girdle	The outer circumference of a polished gemstone which separates the top (or crown) from the base (or pavilion).
Heft	To judge weight (for instance of a gemstone).
Kerf	The groove cut in a rough diamond in which the cleaving blade is inserted. When the blade is hit, it acts as a wedge to force the two parts of the stone apart along the cleavage plane.
Pavilion	That section of a faceted gemstone below its perimeter or 'girdle'.
Pipe	A core of rock that has solidified in the vent shaft of a volcano. Pipes composed of 'kimberlite', or 'lamproite', sometimes contain diamonds.

Scaife	A cast iron lap, rotated at 2,500 rpm, which is used for polishing diamonds. The scaife has a porous surface which is coated with a mixture of olive (or castor) oil and diamond dust.
Sawyer	A diamond cutter who operates a bank of sawing machines, often consisting of up to 40 individual saws.
Table facet	The large central facet on the crown of a polished gemstone.
Tilt test	A simple method of distinguishing a brilliant-cut diamond from a simulant (provided they are modern ideal cuts). The stone is viewed against a dark background with the table facet at right-angles to the line of vision. If the stone is a diamond it will appear uniformly bright, even when it is tilted away at increasingly greater angles to the line of vision. If the stone is a simulant (having a lower refractive index than diamond), dark segments will begin to appear at the lower half of the stone as it is tilted (this is where light begins to 'leak' from the rear pavilion facets). Only two simulants, strontium titanate and rutile, which have refractive indices higher than diamond, cannot be identified by the tilt test. However, both of these simulants show much more colourful dispersion or 'fire' than diamond.
Yield	When a diamond is polished from the rough, the yield is given as a percentage of the weight of the polished diamond(s) against the weight of the original rough crystal.